Finally Found You

A Tempting Signs Novella

CARRIE ANN RYAN

Published by Fated Desires Publishing

ISBN-13: 978-1-943123-05-6
Cover Art by Charity Hendry

Author Highlights

Praise for Carrie Ann Ryan....

"Carrie Ann Ryan knows how to pull your heartstrings and make your pulse pound! Her wonderful Redwood Pack series will draw you in and keep you reading long into the night. I can't wait to see what comes next with the new generation, the Talons. Keep them coming, Carrie Ann!" –Lara Adrian, New York Times bestselling author of CRAVE THE NIGHT

"With snarky humor, sizzling love scenes, and brilliant, imaginative worldbuilding, The Dante's Circle series reads as if Carrie Ann Ryan peeked at my personal wish list!" – NYT Bestselling Author, Larissa Ione

"Carrie Ann Ryan writes sexy shifters in a world full of passionate happily-ever-afters." – *New York Times* Bestselling Author Vivian Arend

“Carrie Ann’s books are sexy with characters you can’t help but love from page one. They are heat and heart blended to perfection.” *New York Times* Bestselling Author Jayne Rylon

Carrie Ann Ryan's books are wickedly funny and deliciously hot, with plenty of twists to keep you guessing. They'll keep you up all night!” USA Today Bestselling Author Cari Quinn

"Once again, Carrie Ann Ryan knocks the Dante's Circle series out of the park. The queen of hot, sexy, enthralling paranormal romance, Carrie Ann is an author not to miss!" *New York Times* bestselling Author Marie Harte

Praise for the Redwood Pack Series...

“You will not be disappointed in the Redwood Pack.” *Books-n-Kisses*

“I was so completely immersed in this story that I felt what the characters felt. BLOWN AWAY.” *Delphina’s Book Reviews.*

"I love all the wolves in the Redwood Pack and eagerly anticipate all the brothers' stories." *The Book Vixen*
"Shifter romances are a dime a dozen, but good ones aren't as plentiful as one would think. This is one of the goods one." *Book Binge*
"With the hints of things to come for the Redwoods, I can't wait to read the next book!" *Scorching Book Reviews*
"Ryan outdid herself on this book." *The Romance Reviews*

Praise for the Dante's Circle Series...

"This author better write the next books quickly or I will Occupy Her Lawn until she releases more! Pure romance enjoyment here. Now go put this on your TBR pile—shoo!" *The Book Vixen*
"I, for one, will definitely be following the series to see what happens to the seven." *Cocktails & Books*
"The world of Dante's Circle series is enthralling and with each book gets

deeper and deeper as does Carrie Ann's writing." Literal Addiction

Praise for the Montgomery Ink Series...

"Shea and Shep are so cute together and really offset each other in a brilliant way. " *Literal Addiction*
"This was a very quick and spicy read. I really enjoyed reading about Sassy, Rafe & Ian. I really hope there will be more of these three in the future." *Books n Kisses*

Praise for the Holiday, Montana Series...

"Charmed Spirits was a solid first book in this new series and I'm looking forward to seeing where it goes." *RR@H Novel Thoughts & Book Thoughts*
"If you're looking for a light book full of magic, love and hot little scenes on various objects, then this book is for you! You'll soon find that tables are no

longer for eating meals of the food variety ... Bon appétit!" *Under the Covers*

"The book was well written and had the perfect setting the steamy bits where really really hot and the story one of sweet romance. Well done Carrie" *Bitten by Love Reviews*

Finally Found You

The moment Presley Mackenzie walks into her kitchen only to find her boyfriend in a sweaty encounter with another woman on her kitchen counter, she vows to give up men forever. Between her testosterone-heavy day job, her broken heart, and her need to grow into her shoes, dating just isn't important.

Mason Sutton not only just got dumped by the woman he thought he'd spend the rest of his life with, but now he finds himself healing the woman his brother cheated on. He's spent his entire life living in his brother's shadow only to find himself wanting the one woman he can't have.

As Presley and Mason soothe each other's hurts, they find themselves falling for each other even as they fight it. But as they learn to forgive and fall in love, their pasts come back to haunt them and the future they thought they could have starts to crumble before it can take hold.

CHAPTER ONE

It is said that a kitchen counter can harvest more bacteria than a toilet bowl.

Knowing that, Presley Mackenzie figured it would take more than bleach to get her friend's ass print off the countertop after the woman finished having sex with Trent.

Trent, as in Presley's boyfriend.

At first, Presley wasn't exactly sure what she was witnessing. Yes, that was her kitchen counter. Yes, that was her friend, Stacy—former friend, now that she thought about it—with her skirt hiked up around her waist. Her now ex-friend had her shirt open, her bra glaringly red against her fake-tanned skin. That same ex-friend had her arms back, her hands clinging to the edge of the breakfast counter where Presley had once loved to eat and enjoy a fresh cup of coffee in the mornings.

She wasn't sure she'd be able to do that anymore.

Eat there, that was.

She'd never had sex on her kitchen counter. In fact, she'd never had sex anywhere except for her bedroom.

With the lights off.

And her back to the mattress.

Quietly.

Trent had always frowned on doing something as improper as giving into one's urges. He liked things done on time, quietly, and quickly. In his case, the latter was spot on every time. The irony of what he frowned on made her want to scream since the man currently had his pants around his ankles, his belt buckle clanging against the tile with each thrust, as he banged her friend. The woman had one leg wrapped around his waist, the other on his shoulder. It seemed her hours in yoga were paying off.

Not that she truly cared how flexible Stacy was.

No, right then, Presley wanted to crawl in a hole and hide. Maybe if she did, she'd wake up and find out it was all a very bad dream. Hiding might not be the bravest thing, but it beat having to deal with this.

God, she didn't want to deal with this. For a moment, she wished she could walk back out and forget what she'd seen. Maybe even go back in time and stop at the store for milk or something so Trent and Stacy would have been done.

Burying her head in the sand wouldn't work though.

It never did.

Trent moaned then gripped Stacy's breast, plucking her nipple.

"Oh, yeah, Stacy. Yeah. Yeah. Yeah."

Nope. Not a dream.

Trent needed a new phrase while getting his groove on—or whatever the hell *this* was. Just saying.

Why the hell was she thinking about Trent's sex phrases while he fucked Stacy? It wasn't like Trent ever spoke during their times together. No, he merely panted a bit before grunting, his eyes closed or off in the distance. He never gave her the same eye contact he was giving Stacy.

What a bastard.

Stacy's blonde hair shone brightly under the warm lights Presley had put in the kitchen. She hadn't known Trent had a thing for blondes. After all, her shoulder-length brown tresses were nothing short of boring. Not that she cared. No, she'd never had a problem with the unruly mass of curls, waves, and straight pieces that decided every morning which way they would go. Most days it was all three. She just pulled it up in a ponytail or stuffed it under a hat and called it a day.

She didn't need the two-hundred-dollar dye jobs Stacy had every four weeks.

Or so she thought.

Nope.

She wasn't going to compare herself. Not when Trent was *still* pumping like a lunatic and Presley didn't have any ice cream in her hand.

"I guess I should have called to say I was coming home early," Presley said, surprising herself. "Or maybe that was you two. Coming that is."

Well, look at her go, making jokes while she wanted to run and hide. Good job.

Stacy looked over, a wide smile on her face before forming that perfect "O" as she came.

Bitch.

Trent, on the other hand, looked over, scrunched his face, and then pumped one last time before he froze. His lip lifted in a snarl, one eye squinted, and he moaned a weird grunt before pausing.

Yep, that was Trent's sex face.

And yet her heart felt as if someone had ripped it out and put it in the blender at the sight of the two people she should have trusted the most on her kitchen counter.

"You're home early," Trent said calmly. He then pulled out of Stacy, took off the condom, and waddled over to the trashcan.

He bent over—so not an image Presley ever wanted to see again—and pulled up his pants. Stacy hummed a bit as she righted her clothing, and Presley seethed.

Why were they acting so calm?

Shouldn't they be looking a little ashamed? Shouldn't they be trying to hide themselves? What the hell?

Nope. She was done. So freaking done.

"Get out. Both of you. Just get the fuck out of my house."

Trent raised a brow. "Honey. Please. Don't make a scene."

"Yes, darling," Stacy purred. "It's unbecoming."

Presley's hands shook, and she tucked them in the pockets of her hoodie. She knew she looked like some grunge reject next to Perfect Stacy and Polished Trent, but grunge was who she was. Presley of the hoodie and jeans.

The person Trent had dated for over a year.

And yet, apparently, he'd been screwing Stacy as well. There was no way from the way they were acting just then that this was a one-time thing. Oh no, not with that cat-in-cream look on Stacy's face.

"I said get out. We're done. All of us. I don't care what you have to say, but I'm not going to stand here and listen to your excuses."

She loved this man. *Loved* him. She'd told him so, and he'd said it back to her, but he had to have been lying. There was no way someone could truly love one person and fuck another person on the first person's kitchen counter.

There had to be a rule about that somewhere.

If not, she was totally going to make one.

Damn it. She veered off track. Again.

"I don't want to see you. I don't want to listen to you. I need you to leave and never talk to me again. Then I need to see about getting my counters replaced."

Stacy giggled.

Giggled.

"Out!"

"Honey, if you're getting your counters replaced, you're going to want to get your bed replaced, too."

Presley blinked, her mind going blank. Her *bed*?

They'd screwed each other in *her* bed?

If she was the type of person to hit another, she would have done it right then. However, she was a Cancer, meaning she reined in the urge to slap that smirk off of Stacy's face and took a deep breath. She would be the better person.

This time.

Then she'd find a way to mend her broken heart.

Because, no matter how much it sucked to say, Trent had totally ripped into her in every way possible.

Her eyes stung, and she forced herself not to cry.

No. She wouldn't give them the satisfaction.

"Leave. Now." Her voice wasn't so strong this time, and she had a feeling from the look in Trent's eyes that he knew it.

"We will talk about what you just saw later, Presley," Trent drawled in that smooth, condescending tone of his. "You're just not thinking clearly. Once you do, you'll realize that what you saw was a mistake, and what needs to happen in the future revolves around you and me."

"Hey!" Stacy screamed.

"I'm so not dealing with this," Presley mumbled and went to the phone. "I'm calling the police in ten seconds. If you're not off my property by then, face the consequences." Her words might have been strong, but she was numb.

She thought she was going to marry Trent. She'd even thought about babies and new houses, and a future filled with his smile.

That damn smile.

Her heart ached, and her chin wobbled.

"Get out."

Trent met her gaze then nodded. From the look in his eyes, she knew he didn't get it. Knew he didn't understand what he'd done wrong.

Bastard.

He pulled a screaming Stacy by the elbow out of Presley's house, quietly closing the door behind him.

He'd acted so...civilized.

So...unmoved.

Her boyfriend had just cheated on her in her own house, and now Presley had to deal with it.

Oh, hell.

With the phone in her hand, she shuffled to the front door and locked it. Then she dragged herself to the living room and sank into the couch. There was no way she'd be able to sleep in her bed.

The first tear fell, and she choked on a sob.

Trent had cheated.

Cheated with her friend.

That sharp pang ricocheted off her heart again, and she sucked in a breath, tears falling freely now. A hollow ache spread from deep within, and she shook, her hand clinging to the phone. She'd call her friends. Soon. She'd do whatever she was supposed to do in a breakup and move on because she wouldn't let this kill her.

But, oh God, it hurt.

It hurt so freaking much, and she didn't want to think about taking that next step.

She wrapped her afghan around her and laid on the couch, tucking her knees to her chest. She'd deal with it all. Later. Right then...right then, she needed her tears.

Needed to let herself feel the pain.

She'd trusted and loved, and he'd broken her.

She wouldn't love again.

No way. There would be no more taking that leap.

Presley Mackenzie was off love forever.

****

Mason Sutton tugged on his tie for the fifth time that night before checking his watch. Again. Where the hell was Lorena, and why had she asked him to come at a certain time if she wasn't going to show up on time?

Well, that was just like Lorena, he supposed. She liked to make grand entrances, show up fashionably late, and be the center of attention. When they first started dating, he hadn't noticed it, but as the months passed, it started to get on his nerves. One moment, she was the soft and petite woman he'd grown to love, and the next, she was throwing her hands up in the air, lamenting the fact she was turning thirty.

The dreaded thirty.

She'd reached and passed that milestone two years ago.

Not that he'd actually tell her that. He valued his life. And his balls.

He took a sip of his beer. His head hurt from his long day at work and the fact that he was waiting for Lorena to show up after she'd demanded he be there. Normally, he wouldn't acquiesce to her every wish, but he hadn't had dinner yet and he was hungry. Plus, she was his girlfriend. If she wanted to go on a date, it shouldn't have been a problem.

Jesus, what was wrong with him? He liked Lorena. Loved her in fact. She'd moved into his place three months ago, and he figured they were on the road to a proposal. Maybe he should have been a little more enthusiastic about it, but he was comfortable with Lorena. He didn't need much more.

Great. Now he sounded like an asshole. He just needed to finish his beer and get some food in his stomach. Then he wouldn't sound like an uncaring ass. He was thirty-two and ready to settle down. Lorena was the perfect woman for that. All soft curves and fire. He wouldn't be bored with her, that's for sure.

He loved her. He couldn't forget that. Even when she decided to keep him waiting at restaurant bar because, as usual, she wanted to keep him on his toes.

Damn it. He drained his lone beer for the evening since he was driving then checked his phone again. What if she'd been in an accident? Here he was being an ass about her being late, and she was probably stuck in a ditch somewhere. He quickly left cash on the bar for his drink and the tip then got up so he could figure out what to do.

As soon as he pulled his jacket on, Lorena strolled in.

It was more of a prowl with the sway of her hips and the pout on her face. Once she reached his side, she swept her coat off her shoulders and laid it over the chair.

"You're here," he said, grateful she was okay. If she'd been hurt when he was inwardly complaining about her, he'd never forgive himself. Though now that he thought about it, she looked perfectly healthy and had, therefore, made him wait on purpose.

That familiar anger churned in his belly, but he ignored it. There was a reason she was late. There was always a reason.

"Yes, Mason, I'm here," she purred as she put her hand on his chest.

Out of the corner of his eye, Mason could see other men in the bar rake their gazes over Lorena's curves. He was a possessive bastard when it came to what was his, but Lorena loved the attention. As long as the others didn't touch and knew Lorena was his, Mason would ignore the leering glances and eye-fucks when it came to Lorena and her clingy red dress.

"Let's get a table, then," he said then leaned down to brush his lips over hers. She turned her head at the last moment so he caught her cheek.

What the fuck?

"Mason, we must talk first."

He blinked. That didn't sound good. No, that sounded like a kiss-off, but she wouldn't be so brazen as to ask him to dinner then dump him in public. He paused, rethinking that last statement. No, making a public spectacle of the both of them was the perfect *Lorena* thing to do.

Son of a bitch.

"Let's take this outside, Lorena," he ground out through clenched teeth.

"No, no, darling. I'll make this short." She batted her eyelashes over the big brown eyes he used to love to get lost in, and he felt a quick slice across his heart.

Fuck.

"Lorena—"

"Mason, this isn't working," she said in a clipped tone.

She stuck out her lower lip then sucked it back in. Mason had no idea if she really cared about what she was doing or if she just wanted the spectacle. Jesus Christ, this couldn't be happening.

"Lorena, let's talk about this in private." The vein at his temple was pounding, and he wanted to pull her out of the building so people couldn't see what she was about to do. He honestly didn't know if he cared if she broke up with him and made him look like an ass. No, he just didn't want her to make herself the center of attention as she did so. Damn it. That was exactly what she wanted.

He'd be upset later about what was going on, but right then, he was fucking pissed.

"No, Mason. I'm done with you. You're not who I thought you were." Her voice trembled for effect on the second sentence, and he held back the urge to shake her. He'd never hurt a woman before, and he wouldn't do it now, but Jesus.

"I have no idea what you mean by that," he snapped. "I'm the same person I always was. You, on the other hand..."

In retrospect, he should have expected the slap across his face. He blinked, working his jaw.

"You don't get to speak in that manner about me. I'm Lorena Van Cross, and you're merely Mason Sutton. Never forget that."

"I'm out of here, Lorena." He surprised himself at how calm he sounded. People had stopped drinking around them, their attention solely on him and Lorena.

Perfect.

Exactly what she wanted.

"You were supposed to be further in your career. Instead you're a *gardener*."

He was an award-winning landscape architect, but whatever. He needed to get out of there. Now.

"'Bye, Lorena. Have fun with whatever the hell you're looking for."

"You don't walk away from me, Mason Sutton. I'm walking away from you!"

"Good luck with that."

He stormed off, ignoring the curious and pity-filled glances. He was sure any one of the numerous men who'd had eyes on Lorena would comfort her. She'd be in her element.

Not with him.

He paid the valet, got in his truck, and then beat his head against the steering wheel.

That was not how he'd expected to spend the night. Not at all.

The anger that filled his mind flared again at the thought of the stunt Lorena pulled, and he had to grip the wheel harder so he wouldn't punch something and damage his truck. He knew he'd feel like shit later as the reality of what had just happened settled in.

Right then, though, the only thing Mason knew was that he was done.

He'd taken a chance on love and failed.

He wouldn't be doing it again.

No matter what.

CHAPTER TWO

Why the heck didn't Presley have ice cream in her house? Frozen peas, carrots, random cuts of beef, ground turkey, and chicken breasts filled her freezer, but not a single carton of ice cream. Wasn't there an unwritten rule somewhere that there needed to be some form of frozen dairy product in a woman's house at all times?

Considering Presley dressed like a man more often than not, and even worked in the male-dominated profession of video game programming, maybe she'd lost some of her female cred somewhere down the way.

Damn it.

She hadn't eaten dinner and wanted comfort food—chocolate, ice cream, mac 'n cheese, more chocolate—even if it wasn't good for her.

It had been six hours since she'd walked into Trent and Stacy making a naked mockery of her kitchen, and so far, all she'd done was curl into a ball for a couple hours then, after picking herself up, she'd bleached her counters before throwing out her bedding. She'd need a new mattress and bed set soon since there was no way she could ever sleep there again, but that was something for the next day. She needed to pace herself when dealing with the betrayal of a breakup.

Now her kitchen smelled like bleach, she had stains on her jeans from where she'd splashed a little too vigorously, and her hands hurt because she'd been an idiot and not worn gloves.

Thank you, Trent.

Plus, she didn't have ice cream.

How was she supposed to wallow and then curse Trent's penis and Stacy's girl junk if she didn't have ice cream?

It still hadn't hit her that she and Trent were over. Not really. Sure she'd cried, and probably would again, but for some reason, she still felt as if Trent would walk through that door once more and make himself at home.

"Presley!"

At the sound of her name, she slammed the freezer door then stomped toward her friend, Harmony. Presley had called her about an hour into her crying jag and left a message when Harmony didn't answer. Considering it was during the workday, it hadn't really bothered her. Now that Harmony was here on Presley's evening off and day of reckoning, everything would be okay.

Or at least that's what Presley kept telling herself.

"He had sex on my kitchen counter."

Harmony lifted her lip in a snarl then reached in her canvas backpack. "That low-life motherfucker deserves to be drawn and quartered. Get a spoon."

Why would Presley need a spoon for when Trent was eviscerated and torn apart?

Harmony rolled her eyes. "For the ice cream, dear." She handed Presley a carton of butter pecan then took out a carton of fudge ripple. "Let me put the extra in the freezer, and we can start talking about the size of Trent's dick."

Presley choked out a laugh that turned into a sob as Harmony rushed past her. "I was just thinking that we needed to talk about his penis."

Harmony clucked her tongue. "We're not going to *talk* about his penis. We're going to say nasty things about it, call it a small, little trivial thing, then curse it so it turns gangrenous and falls off. No crying.

Not yet. Go sit on your couch and start eating that ice cream. The sugar will help you think, and later we can work on making sure it doesn't stick to your hips."

She did as she was told, the butter pecan's sweet and salty taste just the right kick for her mood.

"So, honey, tell me what happened. In detail if you need to. Then we can never talk about it again."

Presley took another bite and closed her eyes, letting her head fall back. After she told the whole sordid tale, Harmony was on her feet, pacing in front of the TV.

"That little fucker," Harmony cursed. "Stacy, I mean. She's always been a whore. I mean, come on, women should go out and have sex. Enjoy it. Claim it for all its own because you know what? We're just as horny as men. But damn it, she trollops around with so many different men, it's crazy. And most of them are married."

Presley set the ice cream on the coffee table then put her head in her hands. "Jesus, Harmony. Tell me how you really feel."

"What? She's a whore. And now she can be happy with Trent because, baby, you were too good for him anyway."

She rolled her eyes. It was nice Harmony was saying that, but it didn't make her feel any better right then. From the way Stacy and Trent had acted and what they'd said, Presley knew this hadn't been a one-time thing between the two of them. That sucked to no end, but there wasn't anything she could do about it now. She could only deal with it and move on. It just meant she wouldn't be latching herself onto another man any time soon. Or ever. Trent had burned enough bridges for her. Now she needed to start over.

That reminded her. "You think Mason knows?" Presley asked, an odd worry filling her belly.

Harmony shook her head. "If you mean did he know what his brother was doing, no. I don't think so. Mason would have told you, honey. While his brother is a flaming asshole, Mason is one of the good guys. A little idiotic with that woman of his, Lorena, but that's neither here nor there. If he'd had an inkling of what Trent was doing behind your back, you can be damn well sure he'd have told you."

Presley let out a breath. "True. Mason always seemed nice, but considering I always thought Trent was nice, maybe I shouldn't be so keen in trusting my judgment."

Harmony snorted then sat down on the couch next to her. "Shut up. You never thought Trent was a nice guy. Not really. You always thought he was smooth. Caring. That caring might have been because he's an asshole who covers his tracks, but that's behind you."

"I hate the fact I let him hurt me this much, Harmony," she whispered, a single tear sliding down her cheek.

Harmony squeezed her knee, and Presley closed her eyes. That sharp pang that had been edging across her heart and into her belly throughout the day slowly faded before slicing again. The rocking motion of her pain made her nauseous, and she forced it down deeper where she wouldn't be able to feel it anymore. If she was numb, it wouldn't hurt, and she could get over the man she never should have loved in the first place.

"He doesn't deserve your tears."

"He's getting them anyway," Presley mumbled.

"He's an idiot. Tell me something good. Something that will make you smile." Harmony picked up the ice cream. "Hold that thought. Let me put the ice cream in the freezer before it melts."

Presley kept her eyes closed as Harmony shuffled into the kitchen. Something good? Every time she tried to think about something other than being cheated on, she kept seeing Trent's ass as he pushed into Stacy.

So not something she ever needed to think about again.

"What did you come up with?"

Presley squinted as she opened her eyes and let out a breath. "Well, at work, they're possibly giving me a huge project."

Harmony gave her a smile and hugged her to her side. "That's great. I know how hard it is being 'one of the boys' where you work."

That was an understatement. Presley made sure she always wore baggy shirts and hoodies over jeans so she fit in with the men at her work. They developed video games and programmed them from the ground up. It was a small, cliquey place where everyone's office and cubicle resembled nerd and geek wet dreams rather than a normal office, but Presley didn't mind. What she *did* mind was that if she ever brought up the fact she was a woman, things got weird. The guys even went so far as to call her Mac since her last name was Mackenzie.

"We'll see how it goes. It's going to be a lot of work for the next few months, and it's just for a bid. I might not get the full project at the end of it."

Harmony kissed her brow. "You will, honey. You're amazing at what you do."

That was true. She wasn't going to deny it. She loved programming and designing. She was damn good at it too. What she hated was the politics. Nothing to do about it now though. She'd just work her ass off for the next few months, get over Trent, and not date again.

No thanks.

Pissed she'd let Trent get through her shields and into her heart in the first place, there was no way she'd let that happen again.

No matter the man.

****

The fifth beer wasn't helping the anger. No, now Mason was just getting pissed on top of hurt. Not a good combination.

His phone had been buzzing all night with friends of friends calling to let him know they'd heard about the breakup. Lorena had gotten what she'd wanted. A spectacle where men would attempt to console her. That slap had been expertly timed.

He drained the last of his beer and contemplated getting another. He had a good buzz going on, but wasn't drunk. If he wanted to be drunk, he'd have gone straight for the hard liquor when he got home.

He still couldn't believe he'd actually fallen for her. He'd done his best in his thirty-two years to be the type of person not to fall for a pretty face and nice rack, but apparently he'd failed in that respect.

He'd taken her pretty smile, fiery attitude, and spark as a sign she was meant for him.

Oh, how wrong he was.

Just when he thought it might be time to settle down, things went to shit.

He remembered the first time he met Lorena, all sinful curves and come-hither looks. She'd broken the heel of her shoe at one of his brother's office parties and fell, literally, into Mason's arms. Trent's girlfriend, Presley, had come to the rescue with a spare pair of shoes in her car. Apparently, Presley hadn't felt comfortable in the shoes Trent bought for her and opted for lower heels to go with her jersey dress.

The two women couldn't have been more different. Lorena, fully sexual with her pouty lips, and Presley, with her sweet grace that wasn't so graceful. He'd never looked at Presley in any way other than off-limits because of Trent though, so his eyes had only been for Lorena.

When Lorena got the heels, she'd been so thankful, so sweet that Mason couldn't keep his eyes off her. Lorena, and Presley for that matter, had been the prettiest women in the room, but Mason had put his brother's girlfriend out of his mind long before that. That's what brothers did.

Lorena, however, had spent the evening at his side making him laugh and begin to yearn for more. Within days, they started dating. Within a month, Mason knew it was serious. She'd even moved in with him soon after.

And fuck.

She'd just have to move out now. His name was the one on the lease, not hers. She'd never bothered to add hers.

Pissed off and a little drunk, he went to their—no, *his*—bedroom to pack up a box of her clothes or something. Maybe it would make it more real and help him get over her.

Because, right then, this emo version of himself wasn't cutting it.

As soon as he flicked on the light, he cursed.

She'd cleaned up all right.

The woman had taken everything of hers, and he had a feeling, some of the things they'd bought together. His bed was bare, the mattress a stark white, glaring and empty. She'd bought the comforter and sheet set when she moved in to, as she'd put it, class up the place.

Her three-quarters of the closet was empty. She'd even taken the special scented hangers he'd hated.

Well, shit.

The more he thought about it, the more he realized how much he'd been giving in to Lorena on the little things because he didn't care long as he had her and they were happy. She hadn't been happy enough if she'd left him, and now Mason didn't know what to think.

He turned off the light then walked back downstairs, pulling out a blanket and pillow from the hall closet on the way. Luckily she hadn't taken those, and he wasn't in the mood to sleep on the bed they'd shared.

Besides, he didn't feel like messing with fitted sheets and the like.

The knock at the front door startled him, and when Mason opened it, the depressed look on his brother's face startled him, too.

"Trent," Mason said as he moved back to let his brother in. "What's wrong?"

His brother might have looked like him in some respects, with the same eye shape, the same color hair, but that's where the similarities ended. Mason was more blue-collar and had the build and wardrobe to match. Trent was very much upper tier and did his best to show it.

"Does something have to be wrong for me to visit my precious brother?" Trent sneered.

Mason held back a retort. He'd already had a really shitty day and didn't want to deal with a fight with Trent since that's what it would inevitably be.

He and his brother had a strained relationship in which nothing Mason ever did was good enough, and Mason, being the younger brother, did his best to change that, despite the fact that he knew it was a lost cause.

Right then, though, Mason didn't want to deal with whatever condescending or demanding shit Trent had brought with him.

“What can I do for you, Trent?” he asked as he closed the door. Damn it, he should have gone for the whiskey when he got home rather than the beer.

“Got a drink? None of that local brewery crap you chug, but a real man’s drink.”

Mason pinched the bridge of his nose and counted to ten. Fratricide was illegal in all fifty states, and frankly, Mason didn’t want to deal with the cleanup.

“There’s bourbon in the cabinet. The same place it’s always been.” Mason wasn’t a huge fan of it, but Trent seemed to drink only that crap, so Mason kept it on hand. He didn’t know why he bothered since Trent never said thank you for it.

“Yeah, whatever.” Trent poured two fingers of bourbon then knocked it back without even wincing.

Not a good sign. Damn it, Mason was tired of dealing with Trent’s shit. He had his own crap to deal with.

"What do you want, Trent, other than to determine my manhood based on liquor?"

Trent poured another glass, this time sipping it. He shrugged, that annoyingly defiant look in his eyes. "Heard what went down with you and Lorena at the club. Tough break, bro. She had nice tits."

Mason ground his teeth. "Watch it, Trent. She might not be my girlfriend anymore, but don't be an asshole." Though trying to get Trent *not* to act like a prick and an asshole was probably a lost cause at this point.

Trent rolled his eyes then took another sip of his drink. "What? I was just telling you the truth. It is what it is." His brother slammed his drink back then poured another generous two fingers. It wasn't lost on Mason that Trent had neither bothered to ask if he wanted any, nor poured him some.

He didn't want to mix bourbon and beer in the first place, but it was the principle of the thing.

After all, it was *his* bourbon.

"Did you walk here?" Mason asked. The way his brother was swilling, there was no way he could let him drive home.

Trent rolled his eyes. "My driver is outside waiting for me. I'm not an idiot."

A driver. Really? In Austin? What-the-fuck-ever.

"Anyway," Trent continued, "word on the street is Lorena is consoling her broken heart with a bevy of men but not putting out. It's only been a few hours, mind you, but there you go."

Mason clenched his fists. Jesus, he didn't want to think about what Lorena was doing. Nor did he want to think about the fact that people were talking about it.

"You came over here to tell me you know about me and Lorena? You just wanted to rub it in my face? Thanks. I already got the memo about her and who she is. You can see yourself out." He just wanted to get some sleep and forget the time he'd put into a relationship that had been apparently going nowhere. Trent could go home or go to his loving girlfriend's house and remain the douchebag he was. As long as he left Mason alone, he didn't care.

Trent narrowed his eyes, looking like a petulant child in a designer suit. "Aren't you going to ask about my day? You always were a bit self-centered."

Jesus. Christ.

"If you're done..."

His brother sniffed. "I actually came over here for another reason."

"Oh?" To rub his breakup in his face? Probably.

"It seems today was not the day for Sutton men when it comes to relationships. Presley...dumped me this morning."

Mason's mouth dropped open in shock. This couldn't be real. Presley loved his brother. No matter that Mason thought her love was invested in the wrong person, he'd never blamed her for that. She put up with Trent's attitude and even tended to make the man a better person when she could.

She was too good for him, but Mason never held that against her.

"What happened?" He also hadn't failed to notice the slight hesitation when Trent used the word "dumped". There was more to the story, and Mason had a bad feeling about it.

Trent narrowed his eyes. "Didn't I just tell you? She dumped me. Through no fault of my own I might add."

Mason saw the lie in Trent's eyes and moved so he stood toe-to-toe with his dear brother. "What the fuck did you do, Trent?"

"Nothing," Trent clearly lied.

"Don't fucking lie to me. What did you do to Presley?" Jesus. He knew Presley was better than his brother, but if Trent hurt her...fuck.

"Fine," his brother spat. "You're going to probably hear about it anyway. You know how people exaggerate. Presley came home early and found Stacy and me in a rather...delicate position."

Mason cursed, his blood boiling in his veins. "You fucked another woman in Presley's house? You cheated on the one woman who could actually stand you with some tramp in Presley's home?"

His brother had some brass balls. Useless balls that Mason wanted to put in a vise right then. Poor Presley. Thank God she'd dumped his ass.

"Fuck you, Mason. Lorena dumped you, too, so don't act all high and mighty. And for what it's worth, it should have been *our* house. Not just Presley's. But no, she never would *let* me move in. As if I wasn't good enough. Fucking bitch."

Mason growled then moved, the feel of his fist against his brother's cheek only somewhat gratifying.

"Call her a bitch again, and I'll cut off your balls. Get the fuck out of my house, you waste of air. You cheated on a girl that is so much better than you. I don't know why she was ever with you in the first place. Then you have the nerve, the fucking *nerve*, to complain that she never let you move in? You're an idiot. A selfish prick. Get out. I don't want to look at you."

Trent rubbed his face, spittle collecting at the corner of his mouth.

"I came here because you're my brother. I thought you were supposed to be on my side."

Dear God, his brother was a flaming idiot. "Well, you thought wrong. Now go out to your precious driver and go home. I'm done with you."

Mason might hate his brother right then, but he was grateful the man had a ride. There was no way he'd let Trent drive home drunk.

"I'm fine, you asshole. See if I care about you and your future breakups. Because there will be many more. You're not good enough for a whore like Lorena, and you're not good enough for anyone else. Oh, by the way, you can't kick me out of your life for good. You'll still have to deal with me at work, and I won't forget the way you treated me."

With that, Trent stormed out of the house like the tantrum-fueled little boy he never outgrew.

Mason ran a hand over his face and checked the clock. Nine thirty. Not too late. He quickly called a cab for himself then ran upstairs to brush his teeth.

Presley was his friend too. Since she and Trent had started dating, she and Mason had grown closer. She might not welcome the reminder of his brother, but Mason knew he at least had to see her. They'd both been through a breakup that day, and sometimes a friendly face could help.

By the time the cab picked him up and got him to her place, it was after ten, and he was rethinking his decision. What was he thinking? She was probably asleep and not wanting to deal with company. Crap.

Before he could knock, Presley opened the door, her soft brown curls in disarray around her head. Her baggy flannel shirt and pants looked like she'd slept in them.

She gave him a sad smile then stepped aside to let him in.

"Harmony just left. We heard about you and Lorena."

Mason did the only thing he could think of. He opened his arms. She stepped into his embrace and broke into tears, wetting his shirt.

"He's a bastard, baby." He ran his hands down her back, resting his chin on the top of her head.

"He is that," she whispered.

He pulled her closer then picked her up, holding her to his chest. Her arms went around his neck, and he sighed into her hair. When he got to the living room, he sat down on the couch, Presley in his lap, and pulled the afghan over them both.

"It's been a really shitty day," he whispered.

"True," she hiccupped back before sitting up fully on his lap. He frowned as she leaned back and over to the table, picking up two spoons and a carton of ice cream.

Fudge ripple.

His favorite.

"I sent Harmony home before we could eat this one. It's a little soft, but ice cream is supposed to be good for breakups."

He stared down into her dark blue eyes and felt something odd catch in this throat. Must be stress.

"Ice cream sounds perfect."

She smiled for real this time then started eating. He joined in, knowing things would eventually be all right. They ate in silence. Nothing important needed to be said right then.

As she took another bite, Mason vowed to himself he wouldn't let what happened take Presley out of his life. He liked her smile, her laugh, her sense of humor. He'd been her friend for as long as she'd been with Trent, and he didn't want to lose that.

No matter what.

CHAPTER THREE

"Mac, conference in three minutes. Bring your ideas."

Presley closed her eyes and held back a curse. It was just like Stan, her boss, to hold an impromptu meeting about something as important as her livelihood. Plus, the "Mac" thing was getting old. She hated the fact they wouldn't call her by her real name. As if, by mentioning she was a woman, they'd catch her cooties. Presley wasn't even a really girly name. It was The King's last name for God's sake.

She picked up her tablet then made sure that her hair was tucked under her beanie.

The little things she did day in and day out to keep the others happy were starting to grate on her.

She was damn good at her job, and she thought that should have been enough. But not here. No, it was the Boys' Club, and she was an unwilling participant in their cruel games to try to keep her down. It didn't matter that she was better at most tasks. Because she had a vagina instead of a penis, she had to work twice as hard.

Freaking men.

By the time she made it to the conference room, Geoff and Franklin were already seated in their favorite chairs on either side of Stan. This meant that Presley got to sit right across from them. Normally, that would be a good thing since she'd get eye contact. However, in this room, it meant the other two could whisper and snicker things to their boss like they were old chums.

Jesus, she was really starting to hate her job.

"So, tell me where you're at," Stan began, lacing his hands behind his head as he leaned back in his chair. The man had fallen out of more than one chair sitting that way, but there was no way Presley was going to talk him out of it. She already had to deal with snobbery because she had breasts.

Geoff and Franklin mimicked the position, and she barely resisted the urge to roll her eyes. Could the two be more obvious about their man crushes on their boss?

"Well, I'm—" Presley started but was cut off by Geoff clicking his pen. The sound went straight to her back teeth, and she winced.

"We're almost done, Stan," Geoff said, that smug smile on his face begging Presley to scratch it off.

Wait.

"We?" Presley asked, her temples pounding. She couldn't have heard right. They couldn't have been that cruel, that idiotic.

Franklin gave her a condescending smile. "We, Mac. Geoff and I thought we'd use our strengths and work together, rather than against one another. Two birds, one rock, and all that shit. We would have invited you to join us, but...you like to work on your own." He winked.

Winked.

Fucking asshole.

And no, she didn't like to work on her own. She hated it. She didn't have the full skillset to design a whole tablet app on her own. Sure, she could do it decently, and was at this point, but it wouldn't be as polished as it would have been if she'd had a partner to help her.

Geoff added, "Stan wanted friendly competition to get the best out of us. Isn't that right, Stan?"

Stan folded his hands over his massive belly and nodded. "That's right. When you two first told me you were going to work together, I thought it was a great idea."

Yes, collaborating was a great idea, but that hadn't been what Stan wanted in the first place. In fact, he'd been adamantly against the idea. Hence, Presley had worked her ass off. Alone. Instead of trying to find a partner who might not be at the skill level she needed but would be able to bear some of the burden.

That was if anyone had wanted to work with her to begin with.

"When was this?" she asked, thinking she should have popped some Aleve before this meeting.

"At the tabletop gaming party a couple of weeks ago," Geoff replied, his eyes filled with that familiar arrogance.

"Why didn't I know about this party?"

Great. She sounded like some jealous kid, but if the others were going to talk about important work matters that concerned her job without her being present, then she needed to know.

"Why does it matter, Mac?" Franklin sneered. "Anyway, we're supposed to be talking about our projects rather than discussing party invites. Really, Mac."

"Right," Stan agreed. "So where were we?"

Presley listened as the duo discussed their work on the tablet app. Stan had wanted them all to design a project from scratch, rather than an adapted design like so many others out there. The role-playing game had to have controls within the design and be aimed at using the tilt and shaking effects with the tablet itself. Her design actually focused on a female protagonist—something she was now somewhat regretting. She shouldn't have put her own imaginings into it. Not if she wanted to win the bid. Role-playing games were notoriously male-driven, and she might have shot herself in the foot with this decision. That didn't mean she didn't love it though. It just meant she'd have a fight on her hands.

Like usual.

Her skills were also more suited toward the graphics and minor programming. Not all of it. Meaning her sketches wouldn't be finished. Not like the other two who could work together now. After she finished telling them about her game, they blinked at her. Their mouths opened and shut like little fat fish under water. She was totally screwed, and from the look on Stan's face, they all knew it.

"Well," Stan mumbled. "That's...interesting."

"A woman, Mac?" Franklin sputtered. "That'll never sell. It's a laughingstock."

"Yeah," Geoff added. "Women don't play games."

The fact that Presley, a woman, a gamer, and a designer, sat in front of them was lost on the trio. So many other things were lost on them.

Screw it.

She'd just keep going.

After the disappointing meeting, she picked up her things and headed home. She could work from there, and frankly, she wanted nothing to do with Geoff, Franklin, Stan, and the rest of the Boys' Club.

On the way home, she stopped by her favorite coffee place for a caramel latte and once again lamented the fact she was dressed like a boy.

A dirty, grungy teenage boy at that.

She wore the clothes to fit in at work, and though they were comfy, that didn't mean she necessarily liked them. Trent had never liked her work clothes, nor had he even liked her job. He'd constantly tried to change the way she dressed so she fit in with his land development associates, but she'd never given in fully. It wasn't until now, with the relationship officially over, that she fully realized he didn't want her. Presley just happened to be the little sister of the famous actor, Ian Mackenzie. Trent wanted her because of who her brother was, not who she was inside.

Her order came up, and not one man looked her way. Not that she necessarily wanted the attention, but it would have been a welcome stroke to her ego.

In the months since her breakup with Trent, she'd made good on her promise to stay away from men and the idea of love for good. She was fully over Trent. She knew her life was better without the egotistical bastard.

As long as she didn't take a chance with her heart, it wouldn't fracture. Again.

She wouldn't fracture again.

The only men in her life now—other than the jerks at work—were her brother, Ian, and Mason.

Thank God for Mason.

She wouldn't have been able to get through the past months without him.

She took a sip of her latte and lifted her face to the sun. The warm Austin air was just starting to get hot for the day, but right then, it was perfect. Soon she'd beg to be inside her air-conditioned house, but for the moment, she was at peace with the weather.

If only she could be at peace in all aspects of her life.

As she made her way home, she thought about that first night her relationship with Mason had changed from good friends to best friends who actually meant something to each other. She never thought she would end up closer to her ex's brother than anyone else before she'd shared her ice cream with him. But that's exactly what had happened. Without consciously thinking about it, they'd become ingrained into each other's lives so perfectly it was a wonder Mason had never been there before.

Since that horrible woman, Lorena, had publicly dumped him, Mason was also wary of starting a new romantic relationship. Though wary was a weak word for the both of them.

They had flat-out vowed not to date again.

Together, though, they'd formed a friendship that worked well for them.

They ate together at least five days a week, mostly in, rather than going out. Sure, it was easier to not have to cook, but she and Mason liked staying home rather than being in public. And if they did go out, it was always to the hippie part of Austin and one of the smaller places where Trent and Lorena would never set foot. Mason also happened to love video games—although she still kicked his butt—and was teaching her how to care for her garden.

Together, they made it work.

As soon as she got home, she went straight to her office. Filled with *Lord of the Rings*, *Black Dagger Brotherhood*, and other fan-favorite collector items and books, it was the perfect office for her. Trent hated it, but hey, he wasn't there. He wasn't present in any part of her house anymore.

Since she'd found Trent canoodling Stacy on her kitchen counter, she'd not only bleached her kitchen within an inch of its life, she'd also gotten a new mattress.

She'd considered throwing everything out and starting from scratch, but that would have been crazy. And expensive. Just because Stacy and Trent *might* have had sex in certain places didn't mean it had actually happened.

Also, she wasn't sure bleaching the entire house would truly clean away the memories.

Bleach wouldn't work on her brain either. Thankfully, her lease would be up in a couple months. As much as she'd once loved her small home, she knew she couldn't live there forever. Not when visions of Stacy's spread legs in her kitchen never quite went away.

With that unhappy thought, she plunked down in her office chair and got to work. She still hadn't named her project other than the dummy title, *Red Swan*. Dangerous and gentle at the same time. She wasn't sure Stan would go for it.

Oh, who was she kidding? She wasn't sure he'd go for anything she had to say.

Not anymore.

When she first started at the company, things hadn't been as bad. Stan had listened to her just as much as he'd listened to the other interns, which, honestly, wasn't all that much to begin with. However, over time, as she started to voice her opinions more and proved her own skills, the resentment streaming from her co-workers had started to sink in. The crude comments and backstabbing hadn't been crazy, but it had been enough for her to learn to hide under her clothes, and eventually within herself.

Without consciously planning it, she'd put all her hopes and dreams into *Red Swan*. The day-to-day stress of the Boys' Club was almost too much. If Stan didn't choose *Red Swan* for the bid...well...

Damn it.

She wasn't sure what she'd do, but she had a feeling it would hurt. Just because Franklin and Geoff had the edge because they were not only working together, but had dicks as well, didn't mean she'd lose the bid automatically.

Presley wasn't about to give up.

She'd put her heart and soul into *Red Swan* and would win because she was the best. Though others might doubt her, she knew gamers were ready for a female lead character beyond Lara Croft. The industry was ready, and there were already a dozen female protagonists out there kicking ass.

So would *Red Swan*.

Presley got to work, draining her coffee and gluing her eyes to the screen until she lost track of time and the rays of the setting sun reflected off the Once Upon a Time mirror in the room, blinding her.

"Knock knock, workaholic."

Presley screamed and threw herself back. Her chair hit the lip of the heavy plastic floor covering that protected her carpet, and she flipped ass over teakettle.

"Shit! Presley, honey, I didn't mean to scare you." Mason rushed to help her up from her tangle on the floor.

Embarrassed, she sat up quickly, slamming her head into his chin. He reared back, slamming the back of his head into the desk and sending her to the ground again.

"Fuck!"

The deep growl of his voice over restrained laughter made her lose it.

Her stomach ached, and tears streaked her face as she laughed at the two of them. Mason raised a dark brown brow, his jade green eyes twinkling with mirth before he threw his head back and joined in her laughter.

"Sorry. I'm so sorry," she rasped out through her choked giggles.

"Jesus, Presley, you've got a hard head." He winced, running his tongue over his teeth.

She rolled her eyes then put her hand in his so he could help her up. "Shut up. I'm sure your jaw is fine. The back of your head might hurt from the desk, but that was all you and your own hard cranium. I apologized, and you called me hardheaded." She narrowed her eyes even as her lips twitched.

Mason chuckled then tucked a lock of hair behind her ear. She sucked in a surprised breath then shook it off. This was Mason for God's sake. She must have hit her head harder than she'd thought.

He gave her a strange look, cleared his throat, and took a step back. "I said you had a hard head. Not that you were hardheaded. There's a difference. Anyway, sorry for scaring you. When I came in, you looked so into your work I figured you hadn't taken a break in a while."

The thought of Mason watching her and she hadn't noticed gave her an odd feeling in her belly, but she ignored it. Mason was right. It *had* been too long since she'd taken a break.

"I didn't hear you come in. I must have been really into it."

He met her gaze. "Must have."

Each of them had a key to the other's home and used it daily it seemed. They could walk into each other's homes without knocking and know they'd be welcome.

It was, after all, not like they'd walk in on the other person in a compromising position.

"So, what's up?" she asked, running a hand over her butt. She'd hit hard the second time she'd fallen.

"I brought groceries. I'm hungry." Mason smiled wide and patted his belly.

She snorted. "First, you're a grown man. You can cook. Second, you could have ordered in if you're really that hungry."

"I wanted home-cooked food, and you're a better cook than me anyway. Please?" He grinned, and she was lost. Besides, she was hungry, too.

"Fine, but you get to do dishes and tell me about your day."

Mason fist-pumped the air like a ten-year-old boy then wrapped his arms around her, kissing her temple.

Presley ignored the little jolt in her belly and pulled away.

"Okay, okay," she said after she cleared her throat. "I get it. You're hungry."

"Thank you, Pres. Come on. I'll help. I'm not that mean."

"Sure, but don't think that'll get you out of doing the dishes."

They made their way to her kitchen, and she kept her gaze pointedly away from the counter-that-shall-not-be-noticed.

She might be over Trent, but even the thought of the image permanently burned in her brain hurt her.

Mason glared at the counter, and she wanted to hug him all over again. He'd been just as angry at his brother as she had been. Well, from the way she'd had to ice his fist that first night, he might have been a tad bit angrier—something she hadn't thought possible.

Seriously, Mason was the only good thing that had come out of her disaster of a relationship with Trent.

"So, what did you bring for me to cook?" she asked as she washed her hands in the sink.

Mason stuck his head in the fridge and began pulling out steak, vegetables, soy sauce, rice wine, and ginger.

"Stir fry called to me," he answered as he put everything on the safe, usable counter.

The unmentionable counter currently held no place in her daily kitchen life.

And that was enough of that train of thought.

Her stomach rumbled, and she cursed herself. She hadn't eaten since breakfast, and a latte for lunch just wasn't going to cut it. Thank God Mason had come when he had, or she would've starved.

"Stir fry sounds fantastic. You want rice or the crunch noodles to go with it?"

"Can we have both?" Mason asked, grinning again.

Dear Lord, he was adorable sometimes.

No, he wasn't adorable. He was Mason.

There was a difference.

"Sure, start on the rice, and I'll get started on the veggies." He nodded then got to work.

"Tell me about your day," he said as he measured the water.

"You were supposed to tell me about yours," she said as she started slicing onions, blinking so she wouldn't cry.

"Mine was boring. Lots of plants. Trees. But no annoying people telling me what to do. So yeah, it was pretty good."

She rolled her eyes. Mason sometimes had to work with Trent because of his job as a landscape architect. Trent, a land developer, depended on Mason and took advantage of the fact that Mason needed that paycheck.

Bastard.

"Fine. Mine sucked." She told him about the meeting and *Red Swan*, being fully open with him about what she was feeling at work.

"Those fuckers. It's bad enough you think you have to dress like something you're not for them. Now they're going behind your back? Jesus. If it wasn't for your boss being in on it, I'd say find a way around it. But fuck, Pres. What're you going to do?

She shrugged as she heated up the oil in the wok. "Work my ass off and hope that's enough. If not...well, we'll come to that when we do."

"I'm sorry, hon." He turned toward her, but she'd just placed the chicken breasts into the hot oil. It popped, splattering on her arm. She winced and pulled back before she fell into his arms.

Immediately, he wrapped his arms around her, and she looked up into his eyes. His pupils dilated, and she swallowed hard, her gaze lowering to his mouth.

He licked his lips, and she leaned forward, closing her eyes.

The oil popped again, and they pulled away like they'd been burned.

Literally.

"Uh, I need to put water on this," she rambled. "Will you flip the chicken?"

"Sure," Mason grunted.

What the hell had that been? No. She couldn't have almost kissed Mason. That didn't compute. He was her best friend. Not someone she wanted like that. It must just be that they were hungry. Or maybe they both missed sex and sensual touches so much that any touch would lead to weird, irrational thoughts. That was it.

He was Mason.

Her friend.

Nothing more.

Right?

CHAPTER FOUR

What the hell was he thinking? Mason had almost ruined the best thing that had ever happened in his life because his dick was fucking crazy. The sun beat down on him as he stood in the lot of the garden center, trying to figure out his next move.

Thinking about kissing his best friend was the most idiotic plan he'd ever had. Well, considering it hadn't been planned at all, and instead, had led him to being a complete bastard by almost brushing his lips over hers, he was grateful she'd had the common sense to pull away.

Or had he been the one to pull away?

God, he didn't even know.

He could still picture the look in her eyes, the way her pupils had dilated when he leaned closer. He could still smell the sweet scent that was all Presley. No matter how hard she tried to dress like a man to blend with her coworkers, she was still very much a woman. All curves and delicious scents that made his cock hard.

No.

Nope.

Not going to think about that.

Presley was his best friend. That was it.

He needed to get laid. That had to be it. He and Presley might have had a moratorium on dating for the rest of their lives, but that didn't mean he couldn't have sex. Hell, that made him sound like a douche. He wanted to have a sexual relationship without an emotional one apparently, and he was all too aware he wasn't cut out for that. Lorena had proven it. He'd been the one who'd fallen for her while she was just using him.

Well, maybe that wasn't the case because he was all too ready for her to leave him without a second glance. Maybe that's not what he'd thought before, but in retrospect that seemed to be the case. He'd gotten over her and had moved on. It was the trail of heartbreak and embarrassment that had been left. So maybe if he found the right person, the right set of circumstances, he could actually have a relationship that didn't include a future. If there wasn't any promise beyond no hard feelings, he might be able to shield himself from any pain.

Not that it would happen in any case. No such woman existed, and frankly, he wasn't sure if he could do that.

So it would be him and his hand for a long while it seemed.

That's all he'd had for months, so it wouldn't be any different at this point.

He had his best friend in his life, and that's all he needed.

After their near-kiss in the kitchen the day before, he and Presley had ignored what happened and finished making dinner. It had started out awkward as hell, but they eventually found their rhythm again.

Thank God.

He didn't know what he would've done if that one moment screwed up what they had. He could rely on her in so many ways, and he knew she felt the same. She'd told him. They were closer than he'd ever thought possible with another person, let alone someone of the opposite sex. He was just horny since it had been a long time since he'd had a woman, so that had to explain the reason he'd almost kissed her.

Well, that, and he'd noticed her body and allure long before she and Trent quit dating. He'd just ignored it since she was his brother's girlfriend and he'd had Lorena.

Now neither of them had that excuse.

Damn it. Nope. He had to pull his thoughts out of what could have become of him and Presley if he'd actually leaned closer the night before and taken her as his.

So not going to happen.

He ran a hand through his hair and shook his head. He had work to do, and thinking about Presley wasn't helping the situation. They were going to have a barbecue later that night with just the two of them that they'd been planning for weeks, and he needed to make sure he was ready to act normal. Because everything *was* normal.

Damn it.

Mason let out a breath that came out as more of a growl then got to work. He'd placed an order with the local garden center for his next project, and hoped they hadn't screwed it up this time. They were a good business and usually treated Mason well, but as he didn't have Trent's money, he lost out on things sometimes. When he didn't take one of Trent's offered—meaning forced—jobs at one of the ritzy developments that made no sense to Mason, Trent would buy out what Mason needed for his own projects, fucking over his current job.

Trent was all suits and ambition while Mason was dirt and roots. It had always been that way, and no matter what he'd tried to do to patch their relationship up when he was younger, it never worked. Trent did what he wanted and used whomever he could to get ahead in the land development world, and Mason worked his ass off to clean up his brother's messes.

Mason wasn't a fucking hippie, in spite of what Trent said, but he did care about the environment and used natural and native plants he found on his own for his projects. When he was forced to work with his brother because of lack of funds and the need to eat and pay rent, he had to do what Trent wanted, but Mason did his best not to negatively impact the environment when he did it.

If things panned out, though, Mason wouldn't have to work with his brother—well, *for* was the description Trent liked to use—too much longer. He'd applied for a job on a government grant out of state that would allow him to do what he actually wanted to do, create sanctuaries and other environmentally sound projects, rather than work for his rich brother.

Of course, that was all a pipe dream if he really thought about it. There was really no way that anyone from out of state would hire him from the vast pool of people applying for the grant and position. There was such a minuscule chance he hadn't even told Presley about it. Why worry either of them with something that might never happen?

For now, he'd put his head down, work on the projects he could, and save as much money as possible so he could walk away from Trent for good.

With that in mind, he went into the garden center and held back a sigh of relief that they had everything he needed. It seemed Trent hadn't gotten to them yet. Thank God. It might be bad business for them to sell his crap before he got there, but Trent was always good about lining pockets and putting on that annoyingly charming smile to get what he wanted.

Now Mason had enough of what he needed to finish his project on time and make a decent profit on it. It was about time that happened.

He worked late into the afternoon, stripping his shirt off in the Austin heat. He couldn't afford helpers and other workers on small projects like this, so he was the one who did all the heavy lifting. Maybe one day he'd have help, but for now, this was his life. He loved the feel of dirt on his hands and sweat on his brow. It made him think he'd actually done something worth doing for the day. He loved seeing what he could do with a piece of property and how he could make it flourish using what nature had provided.

Okay, so maybe he was a bit of a hippie.

Whatever.

“Such a migrant worker.”

Mason froze, his hands deep in mulch. He let out a breath then looked over his shoulder. “Lorena.” Beautiful, bitchy, and apparently racist, Lorena.

“I was driving by and just happened to look out the window, and what do I see? A silly little man with his hands in the dirt. Imagine that.”

Mason didn’t respond, nor did he give her any expression at all. God, he truly didn’t care about her. Not in the slightest. He didn’t hate her for leaving and didn’t want her back. He just didn’t care.

That was a sad state in itself.

“Nothing? Not going to tell me about how plants are life and I need to hug a tree?”

He raised a brow. Was she really so bored she wanted to pick a fight? Jesus, he was so close to being done for the day so that he could go home, grab a shower, and see Presley.

Presley.

Yep, so much better for him than Lorena—even if they were just friends.

"I'm almost done, Lorena. If you don't need anything, I'd take it kindly if you move away. You don't want me to accidently get some of this mulch on that fancy dress of yours."

Lorena narrowed her eyes, even as she took a step back. "You wouldn't."

Mason stood, mulch in his hands. She scurried away to her car, driving off in a huff. Okay, so he wouldn't have thrown mulch at her like some toddler, but it was a good deterrent anyway.

What were the odds that Lorena would be driving by while he was working? He looked over his shoulder at the neighborhood and shrugged. Well, it was one of those gated community types, so really, it was just like her type of place to socialize with women who thought they were too good for the likes of him.

Jesus, he needed to stop judging and get back to work. This was going to give him an ulcer if he didn't let it all go.

He finished up his work for the day and headed home. By the time he finished his shower and picked up the beer from his fridge, he was ready to call it a day and just relax. If it had been anyone else, Mason would have begged off and just hung out at home, but Presley had bought the damn grill for her deck and wanted to try it out. He wasn't going to deprive her of this.

Like always, he walked in without knocking, beer under one arm and a sack of corn in the other. They were going to do dinner right that night. He made his way to the back deck, where Presley danced in a little circle, her sundress brushing her knees. Mason swallowed hard, forcing his gaze from her legs. Damn it, he shouldn't be looking at her legs. Only, when he looked up, she faced him and all he could do was pull his eyes from her chest.

Her really fucking amazing chest.

He coughed, setting the beer next to her small cooler and licked his lips. "Hey."

She tucked a piece of hair behind her ear. “Hey. You’re here.” Her gaze traveled down his body and he felt each lick of heat. “Oh, you brought beer. Good. I’m dying of thirst.”

“Me, too.”

He set down the corn, got them each a bottle, and tipped his to hers in a toast before downing half in one long pull. He watched the way her lips sucked on the rim of the bottle, the way her throat worked as she swallowed, and he knew it was going to be one long fucking night.

Four or five beers in, maybe more since he couldn’t quite remember that last one, he knew something had changed for the both of them. Something big enough they actually had to talk about it.

“The food was good, right?” she said, her voice soft.

He sighed then tugged her closer on the porch swing. “Yep. Best ever.”

She snorted, then giggled, before sighing into his body.

They'd sat out on this swing dozens of times before, yet right then, something was different. Something he didn't want to name, but knew they'd have to.

He pulled away slightly and looked down at her, cupping her face. Her eyes widened and her mouth parted.

"What are you doing?" she breathed.

"How drunk are you?" he asked, rubbing her lower lip with his thumb.

"Mason..."

"How drunk are you, Pres?" Because if she was too far gone, he wasn't about to kiss her then.

"I'm only buzzed. Well, at least I used to be, because from the way you're looking at me right now, I'm suddenly stone cold sober."

He nodded. "The same for me. I'm going to kiss you now. Okay? I just need to see something."

She sucked in a breath. “Mason, we can’t. We can’t ruin what we have. I don’t want to do that.”

He shook his head. “We won’t. It’s just you and me here, Pres. Just you and me. We’re still the same people we were before, and I’m not making us break our promises. But since yesterday in the kitchen? I’ve needed to see if this will work.”

She nodded and he took that as a yes. He leaned down, brushing his lips on hers, once. Twice.

She tasted of sweetness, beer, and brisket. He couldn’t ask for anything more. His teeth nibbled at her lips, and when he pulled back, she sucked on his tongue, increasing the pace and deepening the kiss.

He pulled away fully, knowing they both needed to stop and talk. He couldn’t ruin what they had, not even for something he knew could be—no, *would* be—fucking fantastic.

His heart pulsed loudly in his ears as he leaned his forehead against hers, trying to catch his breath.

"What was that, Mason?" Presley asked, finally moving away. She stood, folding her arms under her chest. That only made him feel like a lecher since he couldn't stop staring at her tits. *So* not the time.

"That was what almost happened in the kitchen."

"Yeah. I know that. I know what we almost did, but we didn't do that. You're my best friend, Mason. I'm not going to ruin that just because you're a good kisser."

He grinned despite himself. "I'm a good kisser?"

She flipped him off, rolling her eyes. "So not the point, Mason Sutton. Why would you kiss me?"

He let out a breath. "You kissed me back."

Presley closed her eyes tight, biting her lip. "I know. I *know* I did. I don't know what I was thinking."

"You were thinking that we're best friends and we do everything else together, and well, why not this? At least, that's what I was thinking. I like you, Presley." He loved her like a friend, but he thought saying that right then wouldn't be the best thing to put out there.

"I know. I like you too. But, Mason, we're *friends*. Friends who told each other we'd quit dating in general. That doesn't mean *we* should date."

He nodded. "I'm not thinking of dating."

She narrowed her eyes, and he knew that was the wrong thing to say.

"Wait. Hear me out."

"Oh, you better lay it all out there, or I'm going to kick your butt."

"Okay, so this is going to make me sound like a douche, but what do you say we try out the other side of our relationship? We're great together, Presley. We fit together perfectly. I don't want to lose you, and if even having this conversation does that, then let me know and I will never speak of it again. Never think of it." *Lie*.

She tilted her head then sat down next to him again. Thank God. "So you don't want to date, but you want to look at another part of our relationship? What does that mean? The physical side?"

He froze, listening to her say what he'd just said made him want to bash his head against the wall. What the hell had he been thinking? This was the one woman in his life who had never let him down, never judged him for being who he was, and what was he going to do? Ask her to sleep with him so they could get their rocks off and not deal with emotions?

Fuck that.

He shook his head then stood up. "Fuck, Pres. I'm sorry, honey. I'm having an odd day, I think. I'm sorry for kissing you."

Fire licked at her eyes, and she stood toe to toe with him. "Hey, you don't get to kiss me and then run away. That's not who you are, so don't start running away from me now."

He tucked a strand of her hair behind her ear again. "Baby, I'm an idiot. Just because neither of us has slept with another person in a while, and we're not looking for serious relationships, doesn't mean I can use you."

"But what if I want you to? What if I want to use you, too?"

Mason's heart stopped. She couldn't be saying what he thought she was. "What?"

She met his gaze, and he saw the fear there...mixed with determination and excitement. "We're adults. Consenting adults. We're old enough and mature enough to explore this facet of our relationship without ruining it. We both have...needs."

As she paused before the word 'needs', his dick twitched.

Oh, sweet Jesus.

"Presley..."

"Wait, hear me out." She quirked a grin at him as she said it. "If we both go into this knowing that, no matter what, we remain friends and we *know* there is no future beyond remaining as close as we are, we can do this. That way, we both get what we need and can keep things how they are. What do you say?"

His mind and heart whirled, knowing there was only one answer that made sense. Saying no would save them both, because taking each other to bed—or the kitchen table, deck chair, and floor—could only leave heartache. There was no such thing as sex without emotions...but he already loved Presley in other ways.

They could do this.

Couldn't they?

He couldn't stop himself from answering, "Yes."

He just hoped they hadn't made the wrong decision.

CHAPTER FIVE

What had she done?

Presley had been asking herself that question for five days. Five long days of work, stressful meetings, late nights bent over her computer, and without Mason.

Maybe it had been the drinks that led her to do what she did. Yes, that had to be it, because no way in her right mind would she risk everything she had with her best friend for sex. Fine, so it would be amazingly good, hot, sweaty sex, but even that wasn't worth it.

Right?

Everything had been fine that night, a little awkward in parts since she now knew they *both* had been thinking about that near-kiss in the kitchen, but it hadn't been horrible. They were almost back to their normal selves. Then they'd drunk just enough to be comfortable and warm, leaning into each other like they always did.

Something changed between them even before they'd spoken. The casual friendship they'd once shared had morphed into something she didn't understand, something she wasn't sure she was *ready* to understand.

In reality, the idea that the two of them could remain as close as they were might be a long shot. Getting emotionally attached beyond their current bonds would only hurt them. If they went into that physical relationship, they'd have to set boundaries.

Damn, she wanted it to work.

She loved sex.

She *missed* sex.

Sure, Trent hadn't been all that great in the sack, but he at least tried. No, not really, but she tried enough for both of them. Okay, so maybe she should quit thinking about Trent in bed while she was working on her feelings concerning having sex with his brother.

There was no greater feeling than letting it all go and coming hard around a man who gripped her hips and pummeled into her. She wasn't ashamed of that. She might be timid in some respects, but she was a woman who knew what she wanted in bed—or out of bed, depending on choice of location.

There was nothing wrong with that.

They were both adults and could separate their friendship from what they would do once the blinds were closed. It had been done before; she *knew* it. Just because she couldn't think of any examples beyond a TV show or book didn't mean it didn't exist.

As long as she and Mason were clear with what they wanted and walked away from that part of what they were doing as soon as it became too much, they'd be fine.

We'll be fine, she repeated to herself.

This way they could relieve the pressure and stress that came with celibacy and their daily lives with each other. They already trusted each other in every way possible, so why not this next step?

Now she sounded like she was rationalizing it to herself, but she needed to be clear with herself, and with Mason.

Things had changed, and there was no going back. If she was honest with herself, she didn't *want* to go back.

That kiss.

Oh, that kiss.

She'd fallen into him, and her breathing had stopped. He'd nibbled at her lips, and she'd sunk into him, wanting, no, *craving* more. They'd started off slow, tentative, and it had grown into the heated goodness that promised so much more. She couldn't wait to see what else they could do with each other, because with that one kiss, she'd seen a glimpse of what could happen if they let themselves go.

She knew he worked hard on his body, not in the gym, but with his job. He was tanned, muscled, and strong. There was no denying he was sexy as hell. She'd thought that since their first meeting.

Now, she'd be able to see exactly what he could do with that toned body of his.

She held back a groan, resting her head against the wall.

Damn it. She needed to get her mind out of the gutter because she wasn't going to last much longer. Mason was on his way over to start their...arrangement. It wouldn't do for her to jump his bones the moment he walked through the door.

The idea held merit though, so maybe later.

They wouldn't be dating; they were clear on that. They'd do what they normally did, eat, play, hang out together, and then they'd get to know each other intimately before walking away from that part of their lives and remaining just friends.

She could do that.

This is what adults did.

Right?

"You're thinking too hard."

She startled and turned on her heel, stumbling into Mason's hard chest along the way. He caught her effortlessly, the grin on his face telling her he knew *exactly* what she'd been thinking about.

"Mason, uh, I didn't hear you come in."

He snorted then lowered his head. She parted her lips, opened for him, but he didn't kiss her. Instead, he turned at the last minute, blowing a raspberry on her neck.

Sexy.

Or not.

She squealed, twisting and turning in his hold, trying to get away. Only he was way stronger than she remembered, and he wouldn't let go.

"I can't believe you did that." She gasped as he dug his fingers into her side, tickling her until she begged for him to stop, tears streaming down her cheeks.

He picked her up and threw her over his shoulder. She huffed out a breath as his shoulder hit her stomach.

"You're a dork," he said over his laughter.

"Me?" She tried to wiggle, but that only made him clamp down harder on her back. "You're the dork. You're throwing me around like a freaking sack of potatoes. You tickled me. Who does that?"

"I do," he said then threw her down on the couch. She bounced and let her head fall back, her stomach aching more from laughter than his shoulder.

"I get it now. We say we're going to have sex, and you act all caveman-like."

They froze.

Did she really just say that?

From the look on Mason's face, she had.

He leaned down so his face was in hers, his breath warming her neck. "I've always been a caveman, babe. You've just been missing it."

"Babe?" If she worried about his words, then she wouldn't squirm under him. Was it wrong that this whole caveman act was turning her on? A lot?

He nipped at her lip then licked the sting.

Oh. My. God.

"Babe. Or baby. Or Pres. Or whatever comes to mind. Got a problem with that?"

She shook her head, liking it more than she should have. "What am I going to call you?"

He smiled wide. "How about Master?"

She laughed, pushing at him. This time he moved away, and she sat up. "Master? Please."

"That's what you'll be begging. Please. Master. All that."

"Shut up," she said, leaning her head on his shoulder. "Like I said. You're a dork."

"You like me being a dork."

Yeah. She did. Too much now that she thought about it. So she just wouldn't think about it.

"So..." she whispered.

"So..." he repeated. He wrapped his arm around her, and she sighed. "It's just me, Pres. I promise you. We don't have to do anything tonight other than hang out, eat, play video games, and all the normal stuff. Like I said before, we're not going to ruin what we have for what we could have. Got it?"

She relaxed into him, knowing they were on the same page.

"Chinese for dinner? I'm not in the mood to cook." She knew what she *was* in the mood for, but that would have to wait.

"Sounds good to me. Want me to order the usual?" She nodded. "Will you set up the game then? We can go beat up some teenagers who have too much time on their hands."

She smiled, rolling her eyes as Mason stood up to go call their favorite takeout place. They ordered the same six things every time so they would have leftovers for the next couple days. Call them stale and boring, but whatever. They knew what they liked.

She blushed, thinking she'd find out exactly what Mason liked later that night.

"I like the look of that blush," Mason teased from her side.

She swallowed hard, her gaze raking his body. Was he always that...big? Damn it. She needed to focus on setting up the game, rather than what Mason would look like without any clothes on.

And there was an image she never wanted to forget.

"If you keep looking at me that way, we're not going to get much game time in." Her gaze met his. "Unless you want to forego video games altogether."

She shook her head. "No, I want to beat that stupid group of boys who think girls can't play. They're setting up a match in a bit if they stay true to their timeline."

Mason nodded, and she reached out to get their headsets, only to stop as he put his hands on hers.

"Let's not plug into the network on our headsets this time. We'll play with them, but I want to be able to listen and talk to you, rather than have a bunch of prepubescent boys cursing in our ears since their moms are out of the room."

Her heart raced, and she swallowed. "Okay." Seriously, she needed to start acting like her normal self because this tongue-tied woman who practically panted for the man in front of her was *so* not like her.

He sat down next to her, his thigh brushing hers, sending shocks down her spine. This was new...and good. Really good.

She took a deep breath and started the game, her fingers flying over the controls even though her mind was half on the man next to her. Mason would shift every so often, and she'd suck in a breath, trying to control her reaction. They'd played together countless times before this, yet this time was different.

By the time the food arrived, they'd won their campaign, and Presley needed a breather. She was overheated and way too turned on from just a casual brush of skin and clothing. Mason got up to get the food, bringing it into the living room, his cheeks flushed.

It looked like she wasn't the only one affected.

Thank God.

"Want to eat out of the boxes or get plates?" Mason asked, his eyes never leaving hers, even as he set everything on the table.

"Out of the boxes is fine. Less dishes that way."

"Sounds good to me. You want the lo mein or dick first?"

She blinked. "Uh, what?"

"Lo mein or duck first?"

Had he said dick? Or duck? What the hell was with her brain?

Mason gave her a slow smile. "We'll get to what you're thinking about after we eat. In fact, let's eat quickly and play another game. I have an idea."

She blushed, even as she took the lo mein from him. There was no way she could eat duck right then—not when her brain was apparently on dick.

He gave her another knowing smile then sank into the couch next to her, munching on beef with broccoli.

"You going to tell me what's on your mind?" he asked as he dug into the spring rolls.

"You already have a pretty good idea," she answered back as she put her fork in his box of beef with broccoli. She smiled and took a big bite.

"Tut tut. Not even gonna ask me if you want a bite? I see how it is."

She rolled her eyes. "What are you going to do? Feed me?"

"Maybe." His eyes darkened, and she swallowed her next bite hard.

He dug out a piece of beef and blew on it. His lips puckered, and she wanted to imagine him blowing on her nipples or even her pussy before he licked and sucked on her. He seemed to know what she was thinking about but didn't comment. Instead, he brought the fork to her mouth, and she opened for him.

He placed the piece of beef in her mouth, and she let her tongue trace it before biting down, pulling the meat off the tines of the fork. He groaned as she chewed slowly, licking her lips after she swallowed.

Who knew beef with broccoli could be so erotic?

"You're killing me here, babe."

"Then finish eating so we can move on," she breathed.

He snorted then went to work on dinner, joking with her about their day jobs and normal things they did usually. She relaxed as she ate with him, telling herself this was the same Mason he'd always been. Just because there was...something going on between them didn't change the fact he was her best friend.

After they ate, they quickly cleaned up and picked another game to play, this time one with just the two of them, rather than a large campaign.

"What do you say we raise the stakes?" he asked as she sat down next to him.

She tilted her head. "What do you mean? We usually bet that whoever wins has to pay for the next meal. Hence you pay today since I kicked your ass this time."

Mason snorted. "I let you, you know."

"Sure, honey. Whatever you need to say to protect that fragile ego of yours. Now what do you mean by raising the stakes?"

"Let's play the shorter games. Loser gets to lose a piece of clothing. Winner's choice." His eyes darkened, and she sucked in a breath.

"Strip video games?" Oh my. That was a new one. A very good and sexy new one.

"What? It blends two of my favorite things. Video games and getting you naked."

"How can getting me naked be one of your favorite things? You've never seen me naked." At least she didn't think so.

He trailed his finger down her chin, and she shivered. "I can imagine it. By the end of the night, I'm going to see you naked, feel you naked, and be naked right along with you, so yeah, it's my new favorite thing."

She licked her lips then leaned closer, brushing a soft kiss to his. "Okay," she whispered then bit down gently.

He groaned then pulled away, licking his lower lip where she'd nipped. "Dangerous, woman. You're fucking dangerous. I like it. Now be prepared to lose and get naked. I can't wait."

She rolled her eyes. "Honey, you're going to be sitting there with your cock out while I remain fully clothed once we're finished playing."

"We're never going to be finished."

She stiffened, knowing he was talking about the game, not what they were going to do next, but she didn't think he noticed.

"Just play, big boy."

"I see you've noticed," he said, palming his cock through his jeans.

Her gaze followed the movement, and she took a shaky breath. Oh yeah, big was the name for it. Dear Lord, she couldn't wait.

"Game on."

She tried to keep her attention on the game, knowing if she lost Mason would have way too much fun, and she *really* wanted to see him naked first. Apparently his attention was just as sketchy as hers because he lost the first round. She did a fist pump.

"Shirt off," she said, smiling.

Mason set down the controller then tugged his shirt off slowly. His muscles flexed and bunched. Holy God, was he always that ripped? That tan? He had a little chest hair that matched the darkness of his hair, but it wasn't too much. He also had a happy trail that went straight down below the edge of his jeans.

She couldn't wait to see where that led.

"Got your fill?" he asked, his voice hoarse.

"Never," she whispered back then turned toward the game. "Next will be your pants, so be prepared to lose." God, it was so much *fun* playing with him. He was still Mason. She was still Presley. All that changed was now they were getting naked. Best. Ever.

They played the next game, and she blushed when Mason won.

"Shirt off, baby. You can keep the bra on, but I'm going to see those tits soon. You get me?"

"I get you," she mumbled then stripped off her shirt. The coolness of the room did nothing to her over-heated skin, which became scorching under Mason's gaze.

"You're so fucking sexy, Presley." He traced her side with his callused fingertips, sending goose bumps up and down her arms. When he rubbed along the mound of her breast where her bra met skin, she sucked in a breath.

"Next game?" she asked quickly, needing to do *something,* or she'd end up under him in the next breath.

"Next game," he agreed.

A few games later, Mason was in his briefs—his massive erection tenting them nicely—and she was in her bra and panties. Thankfully, she'd guessed they'd start this next part of their relationship that night and had a matching black-and-pink skull set on.

Mason ran a hand down his chest, and she sucked in a breath. "What do you say we call it a tie?" His voice had deepened, going straight to her pussy as he spoke.

"What? Don't want to see me get fully naked?" Disappointment slid through her. Was it because she wasn't as curvy as Lorena? Damn it. Why did she have to think about the other woman?

Mason put his hand under her chin. “Hey, stop that. I want to see you naked, Presley. I want to so fucking bad it’s taking all my control not to rip off that bra of yours, suck on your nipples until they are ripe and ready for you to come, then take off your panties and eat you out until you’re calling my name.”

Her pussy clenched. “Uh...why can’t we do that?” Damn, she liked this brazen Presley. She was going to have to keep her.

Mason kissed her then. Hard. He fucked her mouth with his tongue, crushing his body to hers. His dick pressed into her belly, and she moved so she sat on his lap, cradling his cock with her pussy though her underwear.

Finally, he pulled away, leaving them both breathless. “I want to see you naked for the first time on our terms, not because we won a game.”

“But it was your idea to play strip video games in the first place.” She arched her back, rubbing herself along his length. If he would just move a little more, she'd be able to get off. He must have known what she was after because he gripped her hips, stilling her.

"Nuh-uh. You don't get to come until I say so."

She narrowed her eyes. "You're going Dom on me?"

"I'm not a Dom, honey. I'm alpha as shit in bed, and I'm going to show you that, but you're not my submissive. I want you to push back, fuck me as hard as I'm fucking you. If I happen to tie you up, spank you, use a dildo in your pussy as I fuck your ass? Well, that's just part of who I am. Got a problem with that?"

Who the hell was this dirty-talking Mason, and could she have more of him, please?

"Yes to all of that. Now please let me come."

He kissed her then trailed his lips down her neck, his hands on her hips still so she couldn't move.

"Back to what I was saying. I wanted to play to loosen ourselves up and release some tension."

"I have a better way of releasing tension." God, she loved playing with him, loved seeing the way he smiled at her as she teased him.

"I bet you do, baby. Now, sit right there and take off your bra. I want to see your tits."

She nodded, her clit practically vibrating. Her hands went around her back, and she unclasped her bra, letting it fall from her shoulders. She tossed it over her head then held her breath as his gaze raked her.

"Holy shit. I knew you had beautiful breasts, but fuck. I didn't know you'd be so fucking hot, Presley. Look at these nipples." He pinched one. Then the other. She rolled her hips, wanting more contact.

"Stop moving, baby. No coming until I'm done feasting on your tits. On second thought, if you can come just by my mouth on your nipples and not rocking on my dick, I'll reward you."

She rolled her eyes. "Isn't me coming the reward anyway?"

He licked her neck. "We'll just have to wait and see, won't we?"

"Damn it. Let me come."

"Then let me suck your nipples."

She pushed her chest to his face, craving his tongue. He licked and sucked around the right one, nibbling slightly, before moving his attention to the other. His mouth had just the right amount of suction that she could feel her peak rising, her body shaking. He sucked harder, his teeth biting down to the point of sweet pain, and she came, her body pressing against his, her pussy clenching. If she had his hard cock inside her, it would make this that much better.

"Sweet hell, baby. You look so hot when you come. Have you ever come just from someone sucking on your nipples before?"

She shook her head, unable to speak. "You're the first."

Mason was quiet for a moment, and she was afraid she'd said the wrong thing. "I like that, Presley. I like that a lot."

She swallowed hard then squeaked as he tossed her on her back and placed her legs around his neck. “What are you doing?”

“I’m going to taste you. You’re driving me crazy, Pres.”

“I just came, Mason.” She tangled her hands in his hair. “It’s your turn.”

He shook his head. “Not counting, honey. I’m going to make you come over and over then I’ll sink my cock into this sweet pussy of yours. Got me?”

She licked her lips. “I get you.”

“Good.” He sat up, wrapping his hands around the sides of her panties and pulling them down.

She was bare before him, naked, willing, and open. Never in her life had she ever wanted anything more than what was in front of her.

“You look beautiful, Presley.”

“Eat me out already. I want to taste you too.”

He threw his head back and laughed. “There’s my Presley.”

His.

Damn it. No, she wasn't. They were just friends. Friends about to have dirty, sweaty sex. He leaned down, his eyes on hers before he moved lower. His breath was warm on her stomach as he licked around her belly button. Damn, the man could turn her inside out. He brushed his day-old beard along the sensitive skin of her inner thighs, and she moaned.

"You're so wet, Pres. You like your legs over my shoulders?"

"Please, Mason. Please."

"What do you want me to do, Presley? You got to say it. In detail. Make me almost come with what you want me to do to you."

God, she never knew he'd be so dirty. So freaking dirty. She *loved* it. Well, if he wanted it in detail, then she'd do just that. "I want you to lick my outer lips, tracing around the edges. Then I want you to suck on my clit, nibbling at the hood. Then I want you to spear me with your tongue before fucking me with your fingers and finding my G-spot. Once you do that, I want you to rub it and press down until it swells and I come hard on your tongue. I might even gush."

"Holy fuck."

She grinned, though her own dirty talk had backfired. Now she squirmed in his hold, her body on edge, and he wasn't touching her.

"Mason?" Was it too much? Had she gone too far? She'd never talked dirty like this before. Never had a chance to. Mason was different though. Or at least she thought he was.

"I'm going to do all of that. Then I'm going to fuck you hard, baby. I know I wanted you to suck my cock, but I don't think I'm going to last. I almost came at your words."

Pleased, she shivered then almost bucked off the couch as he did *exactly* as she instructed. When she came on his face, he gripped her hips and kept licking, forcing a *third* orgasm out of her.

Apparently multiple orgasms weren't a myth after all.

He pulled away, licking her cream from his lips, then stood up. “Got to get a condom, Pres. Stay right there.”

She nodded absently, her body too heavy and full to move.

He bent over to his jeans and pulled out a couple condoms. Damn, the man had a fine ass. Firm and ready for her hands.

Next time.

He quickly shucked his boxers, and she sighed.

He grinned. “Like what you see?”

“Seriously. You have a beautiful cock.”

“Beautiful?” He gripped his cock, tugging as he covered the length. “It’s a manly cock.”

“Manly, beautiful, fuckable. I don’t care. It’s all of those. Now get in me. Please.”

“I like the way you think, babe.” He reached down and flipped her over so she was on her knees. “I want to fuck you from behind first.”

“Not my ass,” she slurred. Damn, she was still on an orgasm high.

Mason snorted. "Not this time. Maybe next time. I'll need to prepare you."

She shivered. "Sounds like a plan."

He slapped her ass hard, and she started. "I do like the way you think. You ready for me, Pres?"

She pushed her ass back so his cock pressed against her entrance. They both gasped. "Ready."

"I'll say," Mason grunted. He took her hips in his hands then sank into her inch by agonizing inch.

Dear God, there was a lot of him. Finally, sweet freaking finally, he was in to the hilt, his balls pressed firmly against her clit. It had been awhile since she'd had sex, so her body felt full to the point of bursting, but she'd never felt so good. He pulled out then slammed back home, their bodies writhing as he fucked her. She moved with him, fucking him just as hard.

He picked up the pace, his hand on her clit, and she came hard, her cunt clamping down on his dick, milking him. He shouted her name then collapsed on her back, turning her at the last minute so he wouldn't crush her. There was her Mason, caring for her even when she cared for him at the same time.

"Good?" he breathed after a moment.

"Great." Though there wasn't a word to describe how great. How...perfect.

"Let's do that again."

Again. Yes. She only hoped that every time she gave him her body she didn't also give him her heart. Only it might have been too late for that.

CHAPTER SIX

Mason ran his hand over Presley's side, her smooth skin warm under his palm. They were in bed lying on their sides, her back to him. From the way her body moved as she breathed, he knew she was still asleep.

Mason had been waking up next to Presley for four weeks yet he still couldn't get used to it. She just...*fit* so well, and yet he knew if he commented about that, he might lose her forever.

They'd been careful not to say anything to each other beyond what they normally did. Nothing had changed between them, yet everything had changed. They still ate together, played together, laughed together, and now they slept together. He had things at her place, and she had things at his. It made things easier the next morning for work. If either of them thought too hard about it, they would have realized they were in far deeper than they'd planned. At least that's what he thought she thought. Damn, he was going crazy.

Did he want more with Presley? Fuck. Yeah, he did. That scared the crap out of him because he'd been the one to point out that they could be casual in the first place. Only, they couldn't be casual and carefree, not in the slightest. Now he was in bed with the woman he loved as his best friend and knew if this went too much further he'd love her in every way possible.

Damn it. That wasn't what the plan was. Presley seemed way too content *not* being in a true relationship with him, and he was afraid if he brought anything up, he'd ruin it all. She'd run scared, and he'd be left alone like an idiot.

His plan? Keep things as they were until she noticed he was in every facet of her life and wasn't planning on leaving.

Simple. Effective. And just a bit devious.

Perfect for him.

Presley moaned in her sleep, and his hand drifted over her side and up her belly to cup her breast. She gasped slightly, and he rolled her nipple between his fingers. She arched her back, pressing her breast into his palm.

Good, she liked that. He looked over her body and smiled since her eyes were closed. He wasn't sure if she was awake or still in the remnants of sleep, so he'd go slow and see if he could wake her in the most delicious way possible. He squeezed her breast softly then moved to the other one, plucking and rolling her nipple before cupping her fully.

She moaned, her eyes still closed.

Awake or asleep? Well, there was only one way he wanted to check that.

He slowly moved away, gently pushing her onto her back. Her head rolled to the side as he moved her, and he held back a laugh. Presley was a deep sleeper, and from the way her breathing stayed even unless he touched her, he figured she had to be sleeping still.

Well, not for long.

He moved lower until his face was right against her cunt and gently put her right leg over his shoulder. The action spread her for him, and he inhaled. Jesus, he couldn't wait to taste her. He loved the sweetness on his tongue when he ate her out, licking up every drop of her cream.

Mason blew on her with cool breath, watching the way goose bumps rose on her soft thighs. He grinned then licked around her labia, pressing gentle kisses along the way. Presley moaned again, this time squeezing his shoulder with her leg. He looked up, but her eyes were still closed.

Looked like he had to go a little harder to wake her fully.

He moved so he was on his forearms, his hands free to explore, then spread her wide. He lowered his head, licking and sucking on her juicy cunt while she moaned and writhed. He moved up to her clit, and he pressed the flat of this tongue against the nub, humming softly. Presley's fingers tangled in his hair, pulling him closer to her pussy, and he hummed again.

"Mason," she whispered.

His girl was awake.

Good.

He flicked her clit with his tongue, scraping his teeth over the hood. She bucked against his face, so he put one arm on her stomach to hold her down then leaned on his elbow to use his other fingers on her G-spot. The knot inside her swelled, and he rubbed harder, keeping in time with his tongue. She tried to move closer, but he held her down, wanting her to come when he was ready for her to.

Her whole body flushed, and her legs twisted and arched around him, her hand tightening in his hair.

"Please, please, Mason, make me come. I can't take it anymore."

Well, if she put it like that... He pressed her G-spot harder as he growled against her clit. She froze for a moment before arching her back and screaming his name. He kept his fingers in her cunt, fucking her through her orgasm. She creamed on his tongue, and he swallowed it all, not wanting to lose a single drop. When she finally calmed down, he moved up, licking his lips, before crushing his mouth to hers.

She moaned in his mouth, and he deepened the kiss, craving her more than he thought possible. His cock brushed her pussy, and he froze.

He wrenched himself away and tried to catch his breath. "I need to get a condom."

She smiled up at him, her eyes dilated, then wiggled down his body. "Do that. I'm going to taste you first."

He swallowed hard, quickly got a condom off the nightstand for when she was finished making him crazy, and then fisted the sheets.

"I can't wait to have my dick in your mouth, Pres. I don't want to come down your throat though, so when I get too close, I'm going to pull out and then fill up that greedy pussy of yours."

"So you won't let me make you come?" she asked, fluttering her eyelashes.

He snorted and shook his head. "If I come, then I don't get to fuck you right."

"Whatever you say, big boy," she teased then gripped his length. He sucked in a breath. Damn, he loved her hands on his cock. On his body. Well, fuck, he just loved her hands period.

She slowly worked his dick, twisting her wrist with each stroke so she could squeeze harder. He clenched his teeth, not wanting to come too quickly like some teenager. When she lowered her mouth, he groaned. She licked up the vein, her eyes on his. The little minx knew *exactly* what she was doing to him.

Her tongue swirled around the head before she took him into her mouth and sucked on the tip. The sensation sent shockwaves straight to his balls, and he took a deep breath, trying to gain back the control he'd had when he'd been sucking on her clit. She slowly maneuvered him as deeply as she could down her throat then used her right hand to grip the base of his cock. When she bobbed her head, hollowing her cheeks as she slid up his dick, he had to think of anything but the warm, wet heat of her mouth. He couldn't blow his load then, not when he wanted to fill that cunt of hers. She rolled his balls in her palms, squeezing gently every so often. He let his head fall back, willing himself to keep in control.

When she moved the hand cupping his balls back to his perineum and rimmed his ass with a finger, he lifted his hips.

"You do that, baby, I'm going to come."

She let his dick go with a pop. "You can come and then fuck me, Mason. I know this cock of yours." She squeezed him, and his eyes crossed. "Let me have my fun."

He swallowed hard then turned so he could grab the lube from the nightstand. "Use this, baby. You can do whatever you want, just make sure I have enough in me to fuck you. Got me?"

She grinned, taking the lube from him. "Got you." When she went back to work on his dick, he had to keep his breathing even, knowing what was coming next. He kept his hips raised as her lubed finger rimmed his hole before gently breaching him. He held back a wince at the sting then had to clench his teeth again. Holy fuck, she found his prostate fast.

Her head bobbed as she sucked him down, and then her finger rubbed his prostate in time with her other movements. There was only so much a man could take. He let his head fall back, shouting her name, then thrust his hips, coming down her throat.

His body still shaking, he pulled out of her mouth then reached for her. She smiled, looking way too pleased with herself, then crawled over his body.

He crushed his mouth to hers, their juices mixing on their tongues. Fuck, that was so hot. He pulled away and grabbed the condom. "Face away from me and put the condom on my dick, baby."

She grinned then turned so her ass was in his face. She leaned down and put the condom on with her mouth, her lips covering her teeth.

So. Fucking. Hot.

Since she was bent over in front of him, he leaned up slightly to lick her pussy. She gasped, pressing her ass to his face. He hummed then licked up to her asshole, rimming her with his tongue.

"Jesus, Mason."

He growled then dipped his tongue inside her pussy, fucking her and keeping her wet. When she squirmed against him, he pulled back and moved her hips down his body so she could lower herself over his length. She gripped his lower legs, then rammed herself onto his cock. They both froze then moaned.

"Move. Fuck yourself on my cock."

She nodded then rose up and then back down, over and over again. Her ass shook as she kept up the hard pace, and he squeezed the soft globes. Using her wetness sliding over his cock, he lubed his thumb then rimmed her hole. She shuddered then shouted as he pressed past the tight ring of muscle. He fucked her ass with his thumb in time to her riding his cock, both of them out of breath, sweat-slick, and ready for more.

His balls tightened, and he knew he was close. He increased the pace, and Presley shook on top of him, bowing back as her cunt clenched his cock like a vise. He spurted into the condom, coming just as hard within her deep heat.

By the time they were both coming down from their highs, Mason wasn't sure he could move. He slowly pulled Presley off his length then moved her so she lay on her side.

"Wait right there," he whispered, brushing her hair from her face.

"I don't think I could move anyway," she mumbled.

He grinned then got up on shaky legs to take care of the condom and get a warm washcloth. He came back into the room and cleaned her up slowly, reverently. Then he got back into bed and spooned her, keeping her close because he wasn't sure he could ever let her go.

That scared the hell out of him, but he chose to ignore the fear and keep going. He had a plan. Get Presley to fall in love with him so he wouldn't have to lose her when she realized they'd become more than friends with benefits.

"That's the best way to wake up. Just saying."

He smiled at her words, pressing soft kisses to the back of her neck. "We'll need to make sure we keep doing that." He forced himself not to stiffen at his words, just in case she heard the promise within them.

She didn't seem to notice talk of a future because she sighed then wiggled back toward him so his cock lay firmly between her cheeks.

They lay there for a few more moments, and Mason didn't want to leave. However, their day wouldn't permit that. The alarm starting ringing, signaling it was time for them to wake up and get on with their days.

"Ugh. I so don't want to go into work today," Presley said, pressing into him harder.

Mason ran a hand down her hip. "I know. I'd rather stay in here with you, but there's those pesky things called bills and responsibility."

"True." She was quiet for a moment, and Mason squeezed her hip.

"What's wrong?"

"I really hate my job," she whispered.

He sighed. "I know. I wish there was something I could do to help."

"Other than getting Geoff and Franklin fired, I just don't see anything helping."

He hated being helpless when it came to Presley. He wanted to fix everything for her and had wanted to before they'd started sleeping together. He knew, though, that anything he did for her other than be in her corner would only hurt her in the long run. Plus, she was hella strong without him.

That worried him, but he would ignore that for now.

Mason turned her over so she was on her back next to him. "You're a great designer, Pres. You're a genius when it comes to interactive game play. You love what you do. You just hate who you're doing it with. This game of yours, *Red Swan*, is going to kick ass. It already does. You just need to believe in yourself."

She smiled at him then kissed his chin. "You're good for my ego. I just need to stop worrying about what the boys do and worry about my own crap. Thankfully, it's not just Stan's decision who gets the bid, but he's a big part of it."

"You'll just have to wow them. And you can, Pres. You wouldn't have gotten this far if you hadn't already."

"You're too good to me."

He wasn't good enough, but he didn't say that aloud.

"Let's get showered and ready to go. Don't want to be late."

"Okay, but you can't shower with me." He frowned. "Hey, I like getting all wet and naked with you, but we'll be really late if we take time to wash every inch of ourselves."

He groaned as the image of her soapy and wet filled his brain. He rolled over, running his hands over his face. "Go shower, and I'll make coffee."

She kissed his chest, and he looked down at her. "Thanks, Mason. Thanks for everything."

He sucked in a breath then ran his hand down her hair. "You're welcome, Pres. You know I'd do anything I could for you. Right?"

She blinked then frowned. "I know." Then she scurried away, and he cursed himself. He was going too fast, too hard. If he didn't stop, she'd run away completely and he'd lose the only person he ever cared about.

Ever loved.

Fuck.

Mason rolled out of bed, determined to keep his mind out of the constant state of worry and get on with his day. He had to. If he didn't, he'd just push her away, and he didn't know if he could live with that.

By the time he made it to his job site, the Austin sun beat down on him, making him sweat without even working. What a great way to start the day. He paused. No, he'd started the day inside Presley. See? Much better.

With that thought, he set to work, knowing if he didn't start soon the heat would only get worse. He dug at the hard ground, working until late into the afternoon. This was one of Trent's jobs, which irked him to no end. If it had been one of his, he'd have done things differently and not been in the sun baking when he should have been using the landscape to form his plan. Only Trent didn't see things like that. No, his brother was an idiot and wanted to make things pretty and look like they were worth the six or seven figures people paid for them.

What he truly wanted was to work on something that meant more than the money people thought they had to show off. That wasn't going to happen working for his brother. Unless something else changed, he didn't see anything new popping up any time soon.

He would just have to keep working for Trent and then doing the smaller jobs on the side when he could.

There was only so much he could do in this economy.

His stomach rumbled, and he knew it was time to break so he didn't pass out from hunger. He put everything away and got in his truck right as his phone rang. The number didn't look familiar, so he answered cautiously.

"This is Mason Sutton."

"Mr. Sutton? This is Green for Life."

Mason froze. Green for Life was the company that held the grant he'd applied for almost a year prior. They were an environmentally conscious landscaping fund that would allow Mason to design the way he wanted and actually do something for the surrounding area.

The only problem was the place was set up out of state.

Away from Presley.

Shit.

"It's good to hear from you," he lied. "How can I help?" Maybe they were calling him to tell him he'd been denied. It wasn't the first time that had happened.

"We're calling to tell you we've accepted your proposal, and we're very interested to see what you can do with Green for Life. The position would start in four weeks. Does that sound good to you?"

Jesus. He swallowed hard. Everything he'd ever wanted in his career was now right in the palm of his hand. He'd have the ability to actually do something more than work for his brother and make a living doing it.

If he did...if he did, he'd have to walk away from Presley.

They were just friends with benefits though, right? He'd be able to walk away...

Damn it. He couldn't. He couldn't leave her, not with his heart in her hands when she didn't even know it.

He closed his eyes and rested his head on the steering wheel.

"This is exciting," he said, honestly. It would have been more so if the rest of his life wasn't in such a state of flux.

"I'm going to have to get back to you though."

"Oh really?"

Mason sighed. "I'm so grateful for the opportunity. I just need to make sure four weeks is a good time frame," he lied. It would never be enough time.

The person on the other end of the line let out a breath. "Good to hear. Call us back as soon as possible so we can get to the details. I don't have to tell you this is time sensitive."

"Thanks again."

He hung up and shook his head slowly. What was he going to do? If he left, he'd lose Presley...but was she even his to lose?

That was the question of his life, and he honestly didn't know the answer.

What he *did* know was that he'd have to tell her. Tell her everything and pray they'd find a way to make it work. He'd just found her, even though she'd always been there. He couldn't lose her.

CHAPTER SEVEN

Presley tapped her hands on the table, forcing herself not to check her phone for the fifth time. Mason had asked her to meet at the café for lunch, and yet he was late. That was so not like him. Between that and the worry she'd heard in his voice, she was on edge.

The past few weeks had been amazing. So amazing she was afraid what would happen when either of them looked too closely at their relationship. They spent more time with one another now than they ever had before, and that was saying something considering they'd been in each other's pockets when they'd just been friends.

Now they were part of each other's lives in such a way that she wasn't sure she could extricate herself. Honestly, she wasn't sure she *wanted* to get out of it. She loved waking up next to Mason in the mornings and going to bed with him at night after a long evening of making love and touching each other in every way possible.

She loved him.

Damn it. She loved him.

She wasn't supposed to fall in love with her best friend, but her heart had gone and done it despite her brain telling her it was a colossal mistake. He'd told her they would remain friends no matter what happened and that there would be no emotion beyond the bond they'd held before all of this started, but she knew she'd long since crossed the line into insanity.

Her body craved him, and her heart desired him.

There was no going back from that.

Presley closed her eyes, trying to push those worries away for another day. Just because Mason had asked her to the café to talk didn't mean they were about to have *the* talk. He wasn't breaking up with her because they weren't together.

Sure, keep telling yourself that, honey.

Between her project at work sapping all her energy and her co-workers becoming more crass and judgmental with every passing day, she didn't want to deal with anything else that might take something out of her.

Hopefully, Mason just needed to see her for something mundane, and the edge she'd thought she'd heard in his voice was all in her own mind. They'd eaten out countless times before, and it hadn't been a problem. Just because her heart was on the line didn't mean this time would be any different.

"Well, look at you. I see you haven't changed much since our last meeting."

Presley closed her eyes tight and prayed she was just hearing things.

"Presley? You can't ignore me. I'm right in front of you."

Nope. No such luck. The bastard was back.

She looked up, her teeth on edge. "Trent."

He gave her a toothy smile and sat across from her. "You look...boyish."

She wouldn't rise to the bait. Stabbing Mason's brother with a plastic spoon would only lead to jail time, and she needed to finish her damn project first.

"I'm dressed for work," she snapped. "Not that you ever understood that. What are you doing here, Trent?"

He raised a brow, and she cursed herself for doing what she'd told herself not to do. Well, at least she hadn't stabbed him with a spoon.

"I was just coming in for a cup of coffee on the way to a project site and noticed you sitting here all alone. Did my dear brother leave you?"

Presley narrowed her eyes. She hadn't spoken to Trent in months, but it wasn't a secret that she and Mason were spending time together. It was only logical the man would have found out about them. That didn't make her feel any better though.

"You're sitting in his seat, actually. So you can leave now."

Trent snorted. "He's late, I see. Nothing unusual about that. He was always the brother no one could rely on."

She held back a laugh. Seriously? That was the best he could do? It was so far from the truth it was comical.

"This coming from the man I found humping another woman on my kitchen counter. Go, Trent. I didn't want to see you then, and I don't want to see you now."

"You should get over that incident, Presley. Unless you're still pining away for me. If so...well...we could make some arrangements."

"You're an asshole. I want nothing to do with you."

"But you want everything to do with my brother? I see you're scraping the bottom of the barrel now. You had me once, and you can't get much better than that."

"You're an idiot. Mason is twice the man you are."

"Mason is a servant who needs to learn his place. But we can't pick family." Trent smiled, and Presley's skin crawled.

How had she ever fashioned herself in love with this man? She must have had a hit to the head or something.

"Speaking of family, darling. How is Ian, that dear brother of yours?"

And that was it. Trent was like freaking dog with a bone. The man had only dated her so he could try to get Ian to buy property from him and raise his commission. Nothing was done without a reason, and the man was a cold bastard for it.

"Ian is just fine in New York. He's not going to buy land from you, Trent.

So stop trying to get him on your leash."

He traced her hand, and she pulled back quickly. "You liked being on my leash, Presley. You begged for it."

"I must have been out of my mind. Now leave before I call the manager and tell him that you've been harassing me. That won't look good for your reputation, will it? After all, you've already had to deal with the fallout of fucking my friend in my house."

Trent's cheeks reddened, and he narrowed his eyes. "Don't be such a frigid bitch," he snapped. "You're a whore for sleeping with my brother right after you fucked me. You're just sloppy seconds, and I wouldn't have you back even if you begged. And I've seen you on your knees begging—it's not a pretty picture."

Fucking. Asshole.

"Go. Away."

Trent raised his hands and stood before brushing off the front of his too-expensive suit. "Fine. I'm sure I'll see you again when you try to crawl back into by bed. I don't take dirty thirds though, darling."

"I wouldn't have you back even if yours was the last penis on earth."

"Such a foul mouth," he murmured. "You won't have your precious Mason to run home to when you need to get off soon." Her eyes narrowed. "Oh, you haven't heard the big news? Little brother just got a huge job out of state. It's his dream job. Something he's always wanted, and yet he didn't tell you? It seems you weren't worth enough to stay. Doesn't matter though. You never were worth much."

Presley's heart lurched. What was Trent talking about? He could have been lying, but from the knowing look in his eyes and smug grin on his face, she didn't think so. What had Mason done?

"This is the last time I'm going to tell you to leave, Trent," she said, her voice far too shaky.

Damn it. She would *not* break in front of this man.

Trent leaned down and kissed her. Hard. She tried to push away, but he held her close. She punched him in the stomach and broke away. "Don't forget me, Presley. You never could before. You won't now."

"What the hell is going on?" Mason snapped from behind Trent.

Trent smiled at her before holding up his hands. "Just saying goodbye to Presley. You know how close we were." He strolled away, and Mason lifted his fist.

Presley pushed forward and held him back. "He's not worth an assault charge." Sure, she'd just punched the man, but Trent would file a charge against Mason in a heartbeat.

Trent smirked over his shoulder then left the café. Presley stood next to Mason, her hand on his chest. She could feel the stares from the people around them, and she just wanted to get out of there. Her emotions were all over the place, and she wasn't sure what to think. Had Trent been telling the truth? Did Mason really get another job out of state? She wouldn't put it past her ex to lie—he'd done that for years—but Presley couldn't shake the feeling it was all too true.

"Let's get out of here," Mason murmured as he put his arm around her shoulders. She pulled away without thinking, and he sucked in a breath.

Damn it. This wasn't going well at all, yet she didn't know another way to handle it.

"Fine. I need a break from people staring at me anyway." She grabbed her bag then walked out onto the sidewalk, Mason on her tail.

"What did he say to you?" Mason asked, his jaw clenched. Huh, apparently you *could* talk through your teeth.

"The normal Trent crap." She turned on her heel and faced him. "He also said you got a job out of state and were moving. Is that true?" Anger welled in her belly, and she clenched her fists. Damn it. She shouldn't have cared so much. She shouldn't have put her heart out there for a man who told her they'd just say friends, despite the fact she knew she loved him.

Mason blanched, and Presley took a step back.

"It's true. You're moving." *You're leaving me.*

Mason held out an arm, reaching for her, but she shook her head. "Tell me."

He let out a breath, his shoulders falling. "It was a long shot. Part of an environmentally sound project that happens to be out of state. I applied over a year ago, and they just got back to me. I don't know how Trent figured it out, other than he has connections everywhere and seems to get joy from fucking up my life."

Her heart ached, freaking shattered. That sounded like a perfect job for him. His dream job. So much better than what Trent gave him and what he'd been forced to do for years to earn a living. Tears filled her eyes, and she blinked them back. She couldn't cry. That would only show him the true depth of her feelings, and she knew now it was a lost cause to love him. He was going to leave her. Leave her broken and alone.

Damn it.

"I trusted you," she said softly. "You're my best friend, Mason. Or at least I thought you were. If we were so close, *especially* now, then why didn't you trust me enough to tell me that you leaving was even a possibility?"

"Pres, it was such a long shot I didn't think I'd get it. I didn't want to worry you with something that probably wouldn't happen anyway."

She shook her head. "You thought I couldn't handle it." Well, she wasn't handling it well right then, but she'd push on. She had to. "You took the decision out of my hands. You *slept* with me, knowing you could leave at any moment."

Mason sighed. "When we started out, it was just as friends. I thought everything would be fine. I'm sorry, Pres. I haven't taken the job, though. I wanted to talk to you first."

He cupped her chin, and she leaned into him before shaking him off. Letting him go would be the hardest thing she'd ever have to do, but she couldn't keep him from his dreams. His brother had been doing that for years, and she wouldn't stoop to that.

"Go, Mason. It's the perfect job for you." She swallowed hard. "And you're right. We only slept together as friends. Easy to break away and move on," she lied.

He look like he'd been struck, but she couldn't do anything else. "Presley, you know—"

"I know what? No, don't bother. Between you and your brother, I'm done. I can't do this anymore. Just go. Move away and live your life because I know this is something you've always wanted. I'm not part of that. I get it. I won't hold you back."

He narrowed his eyes. "You can just let me walk away? Just like that? I thought we were more than that."

If he'd truly thought that, he'd have told her in the first place. "You were wrong," she lied.

With that, she left him standing on the sidewalk. Her body shook, and she couldn't hold back the tears any longer. He didn't call out to her. Didn't follow her. That hurt worst of all. He'd let go without a fight, and now she knew where she stood. She'd been the one in love. Not him.

She should have known she'd break in the end.

Nothing good came from hopes and dreams.

Nothing but shattered hearts and tears.

****

Mason stood on the sidewalk, staring at where Presley had been, long enough for people to stare, before heading to his truck and back home.

Fuck. That wasn't how it was supposed to go. He wasn't supposed to walk into the café, see Trent's lips on Presley's, and then have the one woman he loved leave him.

Nothing was going right, and yet he honestly didn't know how things were supposed to go in the first place.

Well, Trent shouldn't have touched Presley. Mason knew that much.

Fucking prick.

Before he knew what he was doing, he was on his way to Trent's place, his hands gripping the steering wheel so hard his knuckles turned white. When he pulled into the driveway, he turned off his truck and slammed out of it, anger coursing through his veins.

He walked in without knocking since Trent had left the door open. The bastard was probably expecting him.

"You fucking asshole," Mason spit out when he walked into the living room.

Trent stood near the windows, his back to him. Lorena sat on the couch, her legs crossed and her eyebrows raised.

"Really, Mason," Lorena admonished. "Is that any way to greet your brother in his own home?"

Mason couldn't help it. He laughed. "Jesus Christ. This is just perfect. The two of you are a match made in hell."

Trent turned slowly, that smug grin begging Mason to wipe it off his face. "You're in my home, so you will treat me with respect."

"Fuck you."

"You're so low class and common," Trent spat. "I can't believe we share DNA."

"I can't believe it either, but you know what? I don't care. I'm done working with you."

"It was *for* me."

He couldn't kill his brother. That would only make things worse.

"What the fuck ever. I'm done. You can build your big houses and force someone else to put in random topiaries that make no sense. I'm not going to do it anymore."

"You're taking the job out of state. Good for you. Too bad you're leaving poor Presley here."

"Can we stop talking about that rag doll?" Lorena whined as she stood from the couch. "I don't know how she captured either of you. She took my leftovers with you, Mason, but she's not even good enough for that."

Mason closed his eyes and prayed for patience. Wait, he didn't need patience. Not anymore. "Trent is Presley's dirty leftovers, and considering Trent sticks his dick in anything with a pussy, you're lowballing, honey. In fact, he kissed Presley just this afternoon."

That reminded him. He needed to punch the bastard. He moved to do just that, but Lorena beat him to the punch.

Literally.

Trent howled. "What the fuck, Lorena?"

"You bastard! You don't get to kiss some little bitch just to make your brother jealous. You're *mine*."

"Stop your lovers' spat for a minute, and let me finish. I'll leave you two to claw each other's eyes out soon."

Lorena growled at him. Growled. "Fuck you, Mason Sutton. In fact, fuck all of you Suttons. I'm done with this family." She stormed out on her too-high heels, and Mason put her out of his mind. He honestly didn't care what his ex did. He *did* care about Presley.

Despite the fact that she'd told him she didn't want him anymore.

God, that had hurt.

Trent rubbed his jaw. "Women in this town are crazy."

Mason shook his head. "No, you're just a douche. Even if I don't take the job, I'm done working for you. It's not worth it."

His brother rolled his eyes. "Whatever. I can get someone better. You're just cheap labor anyway."

"If you come near Presley again, I'll make sure you feel pain in every inch of your body for days. You get me?"

Trent snorted. "I don't want her. Sure, she was fun to fuck for a while, but she wasn't getting me what I wanted. I only kissed her to show her what she was missing."

Mason curled his lip then punched Trent on the other side of his face. Trent hit the floor, groaning.

"What the fuck is wrong with you people?" his brother spat.

"You touch her again, I'll kill you."

"She's not yours, Mason. Or did you forget that part? You're leaving her. I saw that broken look on her face. Poor Presley. Alone again and worthless. You did that to her. Not me. No matter what I did, she never looked as hurt as she did when she discovered you hadn't told her you were leaving. So look in the damn mirror if you want someone to blame. It's not me."

Mason sucked in a breath then left. Trent was right, and that killed him. Presley had trusted him with her heart after Trent cheated on her, and Mason hadn't told her everything. He hadn't even told her he loved her. Damn it. No wonder she pushed him away when he hurt her. She had to, or she'd have been hurt worse. He'd kept his feelings hidden so he wouldn't lose her and ended up alone anyway.

Fuck.

There had to be a way to fix this.

He just hoped it wasn't too late.

CHAPTER EIGHT

Fired.

Seriously?

She'd been fired.

Presley sucked back another shot of tequila then bit into the lime. The liquor burned down her throat, but the citrus helped. Or maybe being on shot number three made all the difference.

Whatever.

The past two days had probably been *the* worst in her life. She'd left Mason standing on the sidewalk, tears streaming down her face, and managed to make it home before she fully broke down and sobbed.

She'd let him go because it was the best thing for him. This job was what he'd always wanted, and there was no way she would hold him back from that. Ironically, now that she was jobless, she didn't have that many ties to Austin and could have moved with him.

That wasn't an option anymore.

Frankly, she wasn't sure that'd been an option to begin with. He hadn't asked her to come with him—though she never gave him the chance to discuss it because she'd been afraid to hear it.

She'd cried herself to sleep and woke up with a headache. She'd pushed through and dressed in her best business attire for her meeting with Stan and the company's other representatives, while doing her best to put Mason and her worries out of her mind.

That morning should have been the pivotal point in her career.

Red Swan should have shined.

Instead, she'd been locked out of the meeting entirely.

She could still see the smirks on Franklin's and Geoff's faces as they walked side by side with the representatives.

Apparently, they'd gone golfing and hadn't invited her. They pitched their projects and bashed hers, and gave her no chance to defend herself.

With that last nail in the coffin, Stan told her that her services were no longer needed.

She'd blinked then walked to her desk, stuffing everything she owned in a box Stan had happily provided. She'd looked into the faces of each person she'd worked with for years and didn't feel anything. She was frozen, broken.

When they tried to turn away or act like they might have been on her side, she silently cursed them. If they'd cared at all, they wouldn't have let this happen to her. No one said she'd been fired because she was a woman, but Presley knew, and she didn't want to deal with the legalities of suing.

She would move on.

Before she left the building, she'd taken down her hair, letting her curls bounce around her face. She'd also taken off her suit jacket so each man could see her curves. The curves she'd been hiding because she'd been ashamed of her body, ashamed to be a woman.

Well, no more.

She strutted out of there, her chin held high.

Fuck Stan and the rest of them. Fuck them all.

Red Swan was a promising game, and she would just have to find another buyer for it. She would start from scratch and find a career where her talents would be appreciated. She'd hidden herself for far too long.

That had been a mistake.

A mistake she wouldn't make again.

When she arrived home after the second round of getting punched in the gut, she thought about eating ice cream again, and trying to ignore her hurts, but changed her mind. She'd done that after Trent, and thinking about feeding Mason ice cream that night only made things worse.

Instead, she put feelers out for *Red Swan* with another company and made a list of what she'd need to do now that she was unemployed. Being proactive was the only way to cope.

Well, that and getting dressed in low-slung jeans and a sexy top and then going to a karaoke bar. That's where she found herself now—tipsy and trying to get over the fact she'd pushed Mason away and lost her job.

At least she wasn't wallowing in ice cream again.

No, this time she was wallowing in tequila.

"Hey, you want to get out of here?"

Presley scrunched her face then looked over her shoulder at the very hot, bearded dude behind her. Too bad he wasn't Mason.

Too bad she really wanted nothing to do with men.

"No thanks."

At least men were noticing her. Far cry from when she'd been wearing her baggy shirts and jeans. That just pissed her off more. Apparently guys only noticed her when her boobs were out and her ass looked great.

Well, Mason had noticed her, but she'd pushed him away for his own good.

Okay, time to stop wallowing and sing.

"Are you sure, honey? You look good enough to eat."

Jesus. "Nice, but still, I'm not interested." She pushed away from him, and he let her, his gaze on another girl in tight jeans. Oddly enough, that didn't bother her. She was already numb enough from the events of this day and the tequila.

She put her name in for karaoke then waited a few minutes until it was her turn. A soft ballad came on, and she sang to her heart's content, putting all her emotions into the song. The lyrics spoke of walking away, of letting go of the past.

She wasn't sure if she could do it, but she would try.

When the last chord rang and she finished belting out her lyrics, the crowd clapped and cheered. She bowed, her head a bit dizzy. Maybe she'd had too much tequila. She'd have to quit since she'd come to the bar alone, and she wasn't *that* idiotic to get drunk and wind up with a stranger.

"Little sister, what is going on with you?"

Presley looked up to find her brother standing in front of her. Sure, he had a hat on and an old hoodie covering his torso so no one would recognize him, but this was her Ian. Her big brother.

"Hey, you." She opened her arms, and Ian picked her up, cradling her close. "I missed you." She inhaled his familiar scent, and her eyes watered.

Damn, she'd missed him, and yet this wasn't the person she truly wanted to hug her.

"Let's get you out of here and hydrated," Ian murmured as he led her out of the bar.

"I wasn't done yet," she said softly. "I think I have one good song left in me."

He snorted. "You're a great singer, hon, but you don't need to be doing drunk karaoke."

She winced. "That bad?"

He shook his head. "No, you were good, but I felt your pain from across the bar."

"Hey, how did you know I was here anyway?"

Ian shrugged. "Sam, the owner, called me."

She slapped her forehead with the palm of her hand. "I forgot you used to know Sam."

"Yep. So when he called me to tell me you were here drinking, I came here instead of to your house."

"So you just happened to be on your way to Austin?"

"Actually, yes." Something odd flashed over his face, but he schooled it quickly. He was, after all, a skilled actor—but he was still her big brother.

"What's wrong?"

"Nothing you need to worry about. Let's get you home, and then you can tell me why you're so down."

She leaned into him and got into his car. She'd taken a cab there, but now she was glad she had Ian. He was such a big brother in every sense of the word.

When they got to her place, she went to change into sweats while Ian made himself at home in her guest room. She came back downstairs and sank into the cushions next to him.

"Tell me everything."

She did, and Ian stayed quiet through it all.

"So, yeah, I'm kind of screwed."

Ian kissed the top of her head. "You're not screwed. First, if that bastard Trent comes near you again, I'll kill him."

Ah, big brothers. Got to love them.

"Second, if I didn't know you'd push my help away, I'd give you the money to start your own company as an investment." He held up his hand when she opened her mouth to do just that. "I won't do it. Nor will I make connections for you since I know you want to do this on your own. I respect that. I will say that you going to your old competitor with *Red Swan* was a fantastic idea. Stan was an idiot in not only firing you but in letting you have full rights to your product."

She grinned at that. *Red Swan* was all hers, and Stan didn't own a single part of it. Thank God.

"We'll see how it works out. If it doesn't, I can always go into pure web design and other markets like that. I have the skills and some connections. I just need to actually do it."

"You're brilliant, and yet you didn't give yourself enough credit for far too long. I'm proud of you."

She sighed, resting her head on his shoulder. “It’s scary, but I think it will be good for me in the long run. I wasn’t happy there.”

“I know, honey. It killed me that I couldn’t help. Speaking of being happy, I know you were with Mason, and I’m sorry it didn’t work out.”

She blushed hard because she’d been completely honest with Ian—even going so far as to tell him the whole friends-with-benefits thing.

“It sucks, but this is good for him, Ian.”

“You were good for him. Don’t get me wrong. I want to punch something at the thought of someone using you for just sex, but I don’t think that was the case here.”

“I love him, Ian,” she whispered, her heart aching again.

“I know. I could tell when you spoke of him on the phone before. You guys were best friends, and I’m pretty sure from the way you talked of it, y’all’s relationship was closer than you planned.”

"He's still going to have to leave though. I think the whole idea that he didn't trust me enough to tell me it was even a possibility hurts the most."

"He was an idiot there, but you pushed him away thinking it was for his own good. It's up to you how you want to proceed. If you feel this bad now, think about how you'll feel later if you let him fall out of your grasp because you were too scared."

Presley pulled away to look in her brother's eyes. "When did you get to be so wise?"

He smiled that million-dollar smile. "I've always been wise. You just never listen to me."

She rolled her eyes. "Dork."

"Brat. Now get some sleep, and I'll be right here if you need me. I have a feeling things might just change for you if you try hard enough."

God, she hoped he was right because she knew she'd made a mistake. Pushing Mason away had been rash, and it hurt like hell. He hadn't told her he might leave, but then, she hadn't told him she loved him.

Neither had communicated, and now she might have ruined the best thing in her life.

****

Mason took a deep breath and knocked on Presley's door. He didn't feel he had the right to go in on his own. That hurt more than he'd thought it would. He'd sat at home alone, not knowing what he'd do about his job, but he knew one thing.

He wouldn't lose Presley. No matter what.

She pushed him away because she was scared.

And he'd let her.

He wouldn't let her do that again.

The door opened, and Ian stood there, glaring. "You better not hurt her again, or I'm going to kill you."

"Good morning," Mason said dryly.

Ian raised a brow. “Fix this. I don’t care how you do it, but fix it.” He looked over his shoulder then leaned down to whisper, “Stan fired her, so she not only lost you but her job at the same time. I’m only telling you this because now you have a chance to actually make something work. Don’t fuck it up.”

Mason cursed. “That little fucker.”

“Pretty much. This will end up good though. She’ll find her way. It’s up to the both of you whether or not that way will include you.”

Mason nodded, his heart heavy. “I…I don’t want to lose her.”

“Then don’t,” Ian said simply.

“You think she wants to see me?” he asked, his gaze behind Ian.

“I think you might have a chance if you don’t blow it. If you’re honest. I’ve said enough, so I’m going to go get some food and be back in a couple hours.” Ian grimaced. “So if you’re going to do anything to get back together, be quick about it.”

Mason snorted. “We’ll try.”

“So not going there. Good luck. She’s the best woman in my life, Mason. Don’t break her.” With that, Ian moved away, leaving Mason alone on the front porch.

“You can come in. I don’t know what Ian said to you, but if he hit you, I’m sorry.”

Mason shook his head at Presley’s words and walked inside, closing the door behind him. “He didn’t hit me. Maybe he should have considering what I did to you, but he didn’t.”

Presley sighed as she walked toward him, her hair in curls around her face. Damn, she was so beautiful.

“Why is your hand red?” she asked, picking up his fist.

Mason blushed. “I, uh, might have punched Trent.” After Lorena had, but he’d mention that part later.

Presley raised a brow. “Do I want to know?”

He shrugged. “I was pissed he kissed you.”

“I didn’t want it, Mason. You have to know that.”

"Yeah, I got that part. I was pissed he did it anyway. Then I wanted to tell him I wasn't going to be working for him."

She swallowed hard, and he cursed.

"I mean that even if I stay here and don't take the job, I'm not going to work for him. I'm done dealing with his crap."

She smiled softly then pulled away. "That's good. I know you're better than that. Better than him. And, Mason, you have to take the job. It's perfect for you. I'm not going to stand in your way. I should have told you that yesterday instead of being an idiot and pushing, but at the same time, I'm not going to be the one who stands in the way of your dreams."

Mason cupped her face. "Presley Mackenzie, I love you. I've loved you since you first handed me that spoon. You're the best thing in my life, and I'm not going to let you go. I'll stay here and find another way to work. I don't care. Or you can come with me." He paused, well aware he was taking a chance, but if he didn't now, he never would. "I know it's scary as hell, and we started off saying we wouldn't put emotion into our relationship, but we were wrong. So fucking wrong. I couldn't *not* love you. I want us to be *it*. I want forever. No matter where I end up, I want you there. Please tell me you feel the same way. Please, baby."

She was silent for so long that Mason was sure he'd made a mistake.

"Presley..."

"I shouldn't have pushed you away," she said softly. "I love you too, Mason. I don't want to lose you in my life, and I don't want you to lose out on the best opportunity you've ever had. I don't know what my future holds, job-wise, but no matter what, I don't want to lose you because of it. I'll find a way to make it work. I can do some of the things I want to do anywhere in the world. I want that forever with you too."

Mason crushed his mouth to hers, desperate for her taste. She moaned into his mouth, and he pressed closer.

"God, I'm so sorry I didn't tell you. I honestly didn't think I would get the job, and I didn't want to worry you. That was stupid."

"Yes, it was," she agreed, smiling. "Tell me everything in the future. Okay?"

"You've got it.

"I don't know what the future will bring, Presley, but no matter what, I'm so fucking happy I finally found you."

"I think I found you first," she teased, and he kissed her again.

A Note from Carrie Ann

Thank you so much for reading **Finally Found You**. I do hope if you liked this story, that you would please leave a review. Not only does a review spread the word to other readers, they let us authors know if you'd like to see more stories like this from us. I love hearing from readers and talking to them when I can. If you want to make sure you know what's coming next from me, you can sign up for my newsletter at www.CarrieAnnRyan.com; follow me on twitter at @CarrieAnnRyan, or like my Facebook page. I also have a Facebook Fan Club where we have trivia, chats, and other goodies. You guys are the reason I get to do what I do and I thank you.

Make sure you're signed up for my MAILING LIST so you can know when the next releases are available as well as find giveaways and FREE READS.

Finally Found You is a special novella in the Tempting Signs series. The series is written by twelve authors for each sign of the zodiac. My novella features two characters who were born under the sign of Cancer. Presley and Mason broke hard and loved harder when they found each other. They are romantic even when they don't realize they are being romantic. I truly enjoyed looking at these two and finding a new way of falling in love. If you enjoyed this story, I do hope you take a look at the other Tempting Signs novellas coming out this year. Also, if you loved Ian, you'll find out more about him in Rebecca Royce's novella, Under the Lights.

If you enjoyed this story, take a look at my Montgomery Ink, Redwood Pack, Talon Pack, Holiday Montana, and Dante's Circle series!!

Thank you so much for going on this journey with me and I do hope you enjoyed my Tempting Signs story. Without you readers, I wouldn't be where I am today.

Thank you again for reading and I do hope to see you again.

Carrie Ann

About this Author

New York Times and USA Today Bestselling Author Carrie Ann Ryan never thought she'd be a writer. Not really. No, she loved math and science and even went on to graduate school in chemistry. Yes, she read as a kid and devoured teen fiction and Harry Potter, but it wasn't until someone handed her a romance book in her late teens that she realized that there was something out there just for her. When another author suggested she use the voices in her head for good and not evil, The Redwood Pack and all her other stories were born.

Carrie Ann is a bestselling author of over twenty novels and novellas and has so much more on her mind (and on her spreadsheets *grins*) that she isn't planning on giving up her dream anytime soon.

www.CarrieAnnRyan.com

Also from this Author

Now Available:

Redwood Pack Series:
An Alpha's Path
A Taste for a Mate
Trinity Bound
A Night Away
Enforcer's Redemption
Blurred Expectations
Forgiveness
Shattered Emotions
Hidden Destiny
A Beta's Haven
Fighting Fate
Loving the Omega
The Hunted Heart
Wicked Wolf

The Talon Pack (Following the Redwood Pack Series)
Tattered Loyalties

The Redwood Pack Volumes:
Redwood Pack Vol 1
Redwood Pack Vol 2
Redwood Pack Vol 3
Redwood Pack Vol 4
Redwood Pack Vol 5
Redwood Pack Vol 6

Dante's Circle Series:
Dust of My Wings
Her Warriors' Three Wishes
An Unlucky Moon
His Choice
Tangled Innocence
Fierce Enchantment

Montgomery Ink:
Ink Inspired
Ink Reunited
Delicate Ink
Forever Ink
Tempting Boundaries
Harder than Words

Holiday, Montana Series:
Charmed Spirits
Santa's Executive
Finding Abigail
Her Lucky Love
Dreams of Ivory

Coming Soon:

Talon Pack (Part of the Redwood Pack World)
An Alpha's Choice
Mated in Mist

Dante's Circle:
Fallen for Alphas
An Immortal's Song

Montgomery Ink:
Written in Ink

The Branded Pack Series:
(Written with Alexandra Ivy)
Stolen and Forgiven
Abandoned and Unseen

Tempting Signs Series

Make sure you read the complete Tempting Signs Series from Fated Desires
Each title will be released in 2015 and 2016 during the time of their Zodiac Sign

Aries:
Lust Actually
By Heather Long

Taurus:
Forever Devoted
By Virginia Nelson

Gemini:
Gemini Rising
By Ranae Rose

Cancer:
Finally Found You
By Carrie Ann Ryan

Leo:
Before the Rain
By JoAnna Kenrick

Virgo:
Under the Lights
By Rebecca Royce

Libra:
All's Fair
By Kate Richards

Scorpio:
Dark Sky
By Katalina Leon

Sagittarius:
Into the Night
By Virginia Cavanaugh

Capricorn:
Her Captain
By Taryn Kincaid

Aquarius:
Buried
By Cassandra Carr

Pieces:
Once Upon a Fantasy
By Lia Davis

Made in the USA
Lexington, KY
21 June 2015